Eastern Oklahoma District Library System

Eufaula Memorial Library
301 S. FIRST STREET
EUFAULA, OK 74432

BARK OF NIGHT

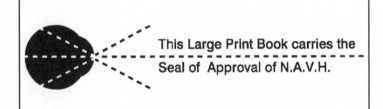

This Large Print Book carries the
Seal of Approval of N.A.V.H.

BARK OF NIGHT

DAVID ROSENFELT

THORNDIKE PRESS
A part of Gale, a Cengage Company

Farmington Hills, Mich • San Francisco • New York • Waterville, Maine
Meriden, Conn • Mason, Ohio • Chicago

Copyright © 2019 by Tara Productions, Inc.
An Andy Carpenter Mystery.
Thorndike Press, a part of Gale, a Cengage Company.

Thorndike Press® Large Print Core.
The text of this Large Print edition is unabridged.
Other aspects of the book may vary from the original edition.
Set in 16 pt. Plantin.

LIBRARY OF CONGRESS CIP DATA ON FILE.
CATALOGUING IN PUBLICATION FOR THIS BOOK
IS AVAILABLE FROM THE LIBRARY OF CONGRESS

ISBN-13: 978-1-4328-7036-2 (hardcover alk. paper)

Published in 2019 by arrangement with Macmillan Publishing Group, LLC/St. Martin's Publishing Group

Printed in Mexico
1 2 3 4 5 6 7 23 22 21 20 19

BARK OF NIGHT

Frank Silvio checked into the hotel under an assumed name, using fake identification.

It had been so long since he used his real name that he was in danger of forgetting it. The truth was that it had no real meaning for him anyway, since he was never going to be Frank Silvio again.

Frank Silvio, for all intents and purposes, and in the eyes of everyone, was dead.

So Silvio chose to be known to everyone in the operation simply as Mister. That's how he wanted it, and he had the money, so that's how it would be. No one he dealt with was about to complain.

The hotel was a Hilton at the Tampa airport. Clean, modern, with a number of amenities that he would never use, other than room service and, of course, wireless internet. He was there for entertainment — a specific entertainment, which he had already arranged for.

He checked in at two o'clock in the afternoon. He had a small bag with him, but did not bother to unpack, since he would not be staying overnight. He also would not be going back out until it was time to leave. Even though he had substantially changed his appearance, Silvio was fairly well-known in this area, and he could not afford to be seen and recognized.

So all he did was order a shrimp cocktail and a steak sandwich; there would be time to eat before the show started at around three thirty.

At precisely that time, he opened the webcam app on his iPad, and the video appeared immediately. It was from a camera on a boat offshore near a town called Wilton Key, Florida, about forty-five miles north of Tampa.

There were four people on the boat, all of whom he recognized. That was no surprise; he had met with three of them in secret earlier that day. He had left them with very specific instructions, which they were now about to follow.

One of the four men was not currently recognizable, mainly because he was in a full diving suit. It was made of neoprene, which meant the helmet was not the old metal kind. But it was airtight and impregnable, which was all that was important. His air supply would come from the hose attached to the processor on the ship. That man's name was Vincent Grobin.

Silvio watched Grobin as he was helped into the water by the others, who then waited until he reached the desired depth. When enough time had passed, they seemed to hesitate, as if frozen in place, unsure what to do.

It was as if they were waiting for a signal from Silvio, but, of course, while he could see them, they could not see him. It didn't matter anyway, since he had already told them exactly what to do.

There wasn't really a hierarchy among the men on the boat, though the unofficial captain was probably Bryce Dorsey. The others looked to him for most things, and this would certainly be no exception.

Dorsey went to the edge of the boat and looked down into the water. Even though the water was fairly clear, there was no way he could see all the way down to where Grobin was, but he certainly knew Grobin was on the end of the air hose.

Dorsey looked toward the webcam, in a silent signal that was both an acknowledgment and a concession. Then he walked over to a table, picked up a knife, and, with a slashing, explosive movement, cut Grobin's air hose.

No one could see it, but every man on that boat, as well as Silvio, watching from the hotel, knew what had just happened.

The air supply, which was pressuring the suit against the tremendous pressure of the water, was cut off. Grobin's body was actually crushed and forced upward toward his helmet. Had there been more room, his entire body would have been squashed into his helmet.

But Grobin knew none of that; he died instantly from the depressurization when the tube was cut.

Dorsey once again gave a slight, silent nod to the webcam and Silvio. It had been a difficult act for him to undertake; Grobin was a friend, but he had inadvertently betrayed them and put their operation at risk. Dorsey might have found another way to handle it, but Silvio had the money.

Silvio, for his part, took no great pleasure in what had happened; nor did he feel any regret. It was a business transaction; he and everyone on that boat knew it.

All Silvio did was shut down his iPad, leave the room, and head for the airport.

"Andy, can I talk to you in my office?"

Taken out of context, that question may not sound like a big deal. In context, spoken by Dr. Dan Dowling, it is the most frightening question I have ever heard.

Dowling is my veterinarian, and I am here today because Tara, my wonderful, extraordinary, remarkable golden retriever and closest of friends, has a lump on her side. He had said that it was very likely nothing to worry about, though of course I was and am plenty worried. So I've brought Tara here, and she has been in the back getting an aspirate done on the offending lump.

But now he wants to talk to me, and the request was spoken in a very serious tone. And why in his office? I've never been in his office; I didn't even know he had a goddamn office.

I make a decision as I follow him back there. If he says anything negative about

11

Tara's health, I am going to strangle him right there in the office I didn't know he had, and then feed pieces of his body to the fish in the aquarium he has in the waiting area.

And that still wouldn't make us even.

I follow him into the office and see that there is another dog in there, on a leash attached to a drawer handle on his desk. What the hell is going on? Is this a therapy dog designed to ease my pain at what I am going to hear?

The dog is a French bulldog and seems a bit agitated. He can't be more than twenty-five pounds; if Dr. Dowling thinks this dog will protect him from me, he is sorely mistaken.

"I have a bit of a situation here," Dowling says. "And I thought you might be able to help."

He wants my help? What the hell is he talking about?

"What the hell are you talking about? Is Tara okay?"

"What? Oh, she's fine. But —"

"But what? She's fine but she's not fine?" There is a definite possibility that my head is going to explode.

"Andy, she's really fine. It was a lipoma, just fatty tissue. No need to remove it; no need to do anything. I promise you, she's fine."

I feel the tension come out of me in a rush, like when you let the air out of a balloon you've just blown up, before tying it shut. I'm expecting my body to be like the balloon and fly wildly around the room. "You scared me half to death," I say.

"I'm sorry; I didn't mean to. I wanted to talk to you about this dog. His name is Truman."

I'm guessing that he wants me to find Truman a home, for whatever reason. When I'm not working as a defense attorney, my friend Willie Miller and I run the Tara Foundation, a rescue group named after the dog who only has a lipoma and is fine . . . really fine.

"What about him?" I ask.

"It's sort of a long story. Yesterday morning a guy brought him in and spoke to Debra, our new receptionist. She said he was maybe mid-forties, a big guy, somewhat intimidating. He said the dog's name was Buster and that he wanted Buster euthanized, but wouldn't say why."

"I thought his name was Truman?"

"I'm getting there," Dowling says. "The guy signed a form authorizing the euthanasia and paid in cash. In those situations,

Debra is supposed to find out why the owner wants it done, but as I said, he was somewhat intimidating, and she's new, so . . ."

"Is Buster or Truman healthy?" I ask.

"Yes. I ran bloodwork and did a full examination. He's perfectly healthy, actually well cared for."

"So give him to us; we'll easily find him a good home, better than he had with that asshole."

"It's more complicated than that. Once the client signs the form and pays, and we accept the money, we have a legal obligation to euthanize the dog."

"So you're asking me as a lawyer what to do? Okay, here's my considered legal advice: don't kill the dog; give him to us. You can't kill an innocent, healthy dog. I won't tell anyone, and I promise I'll defend you all the way until they strap you into the electric chair."

He doesn't smile. "I haven't gotten to the complicated part yet," he says. "I tried to get in touch with the man, to get permission to re-home the dog. I knew you could do that easily. The thing is, as best I can tell, he gave a fake name and address."

"Good. That makes it even easier. Where is the document he signed?"

"In my safe."

"Would the guy have a copy?" I ask.

"No, we just have the client sign for our own protection, so they can't say later on that they never authorized it. As long as we have the original, we're protected. But I still haven't gotten to the complicated part."

I've now decided that I'm just going to sit, relax, and wait to hear the complications, rather than interrupt. There's no urgency and no stress; no matter how this conversation ends, Tara is still going to be fine, really fine.

"Truman has a chip in him," he says. "I scanned it, which is how I know his name is really Truman. It also listed a name, address, and phone number for the owner, which is not the name and address the man who dropped him off wrote down."

"So the dog is stolen?" I ask.

"I can't answer that. I tried calling the phone number the chip gave me, which is an Ohio number, but there was no answer."

"Did you leave a message?"

"I did, but that doesn't matter. He's not going to call back."

"How do you know that?"

"He was murdered Wednesday night. Right here in New Jersey."

15

I know it sounds crazy, but a murder was committed less than half a mile from my house two nights ago, and I am only vaguely aware of it. And to make it even stranger, my profession is sort of a criminal defense attorney.

I say "sort of" because I've been trying to retire from that profession for quite a while now. I am ready to pull the career plug — actually, more than ready — but I can't seem to manage it. I have been getting drawn into cases for a variety of reasons, none of which involve a work ethic or a desire to be a productive member of society.

I am independently wealthy, the result of a large inheritance and many of the afore-mentioned cases, most of which have been lucrative. And since I have never been a huge fan of lawyering, I'd much prefer to stay home with my wife, Laurie Collins; our son, Ricky; our two dogs, the aforemen-

16

tioned Tara and our basset hound, Sebastian; and my TV remote controls.

I have been taking the approach that if I don't watch the local news or read the local paper, then I won't know about crimes that are committed. And if I don't know about those crimes, how can I represent the people accused of committing them?

Yes, I am aware that this reasoning makes almost no sense at all. But it's been working out for the last three months, so I have not been rocking the boat, or watching the local news, or reading the paper. The main reason I even vaguely know about this particular murder is that Laurie was in bed watching the news when I happened to come out of the bathroom after brushing my teeth. I heard the basics but got out of there without hearing all the details, so I figured I was safe.

The other way I sort of heard about the murder was last night at Charlie's Sports Bar. I attend on a semiregular basis and sit with my friends Vince Sanders, editor of the local newspaper that I no longer read, and Pete Stanton, captain in charge of the Homicide Division of the Paterson Police Force. Pete investigates the homicides that I don't let myself read or hear about.

Suffice it to say, all we talk about at

Charlie's is sports.

When I arrived, Pete was not there, a somewhat shocking development. I always pick up the tab for dinner and beer, and Pete would never miss a free meal, no matter what. If I had to guess, he probably doesn't even have a refrigerator or stove in his house.

When I asked Vince where Pete was, he said, "Something about that murder." I quickly changed the conversational subject to the Mets, which is only slightly less depressing than murder.

But now that Dr. Dowling has sought my help, I have no choice but to find out what happened. I learned from Vince that Truman's real owner, who will now and forever be known as a murder victim, is James Haley. He was living in a small house on Thirty-ninth Street in Paterson, New Jersey. I live on Forty-second Street, but also a number of blocks to the south.

The shooting took place inside the house; it is believed that the killer came in through the back door. Neighbors said that Haley had moved in only recently; they believed he was renting the place. They also said he had a dog, and since the dog was missing, it was speculated that he might have run off through the open back door after the murderer left.

Of course, the media has no way of knowing that the dog, a French bulldog named Truman, is sitting in Dr. Dowling's office.

Haley was from Columbus, Ohio, and is said to have been a documentary filmmaker. His current project was a film about urban blight, which sounds like it would have been a laugh riot.

I love Paterson; I grew up here and will never move. But I have to admit that it would not be out of place in a film about urban blight. In fact, if I were to look deeply into Paterson's history, I imagine it was actually discovered by a settler named Urban Blight. The idiot son of Nehemiah and Rebecca Blight, Urban set out with his horse and wagon to journey south to Asbury Park, in the hope of meeting Bruce Springsteen's ancestors.

Urban's horse, who was clearly the brains of the family, decided that Urban's was a wagon he did not want to be hitched to and ran off. So Urban was stuck in place, and that place was the region eventually to be known as Paterson.

But my imagination and I digress.

I've promised that I'll help Dr. Dowling navigate this situation; it's sort of a way to thank him for telling me that Tara is going to be fine . . . really fine. It's also not exactly a heavy lift and won't put much stress on my lawyering muscles, atrophied though they may be.

In the morning, I call Pete Stanton and leave word that it's important, so he calls me back in ten minutes. "This better be good," he says. "I'm a little busy."

"I have some information about the murder on Thirty-ninth Street the other night."

"That was fast. We just made the arrest and you've already got the kid as a client? You might as well drop him; he can probably pay what you're worth, but not what you charge."

"The kid? How old is the guy you arrested?"

"Twenty."

"What's his name?" I ask.

"Let it go. I'm telling you, he can barely afford the public defender."

"What's his name, Pete? Is it top secret?"

"Joey Gamble."

"Pete, this could be important. You need to hear what we have to say."

" 'We'? Who's 'we'?"

"My client and I. When can we come in?" I ask.

He sighs an exaggerated sigh. "Come in

now. Let's get this over with."

"No good. He's neutering a dog."

"I'm not even going to respond to that," he says. "How about four o'clock?"

"We'll be there."

The call came in to Clifton PD at 6:45 A.M.

A neighborhood resident, walking his two dogs in Nash Park, had come upon a body loosely covered with shrubbery. More accurately, his dogs discovered the body, but he was the one who appropriately freaked out and called 911.

The victim, identified as Christopher Tolbert, was a homeless man who had a few minor arrests for vagrancy. A cousin would later come forward and tell the story of how Tolbert's life had deteriorated after he lost his job and home, and how he cut himself off from his family and friends and took to the streets.

Efforts to intervene had been for naught, and those family and friends had gradually and completely lost touch with him.

No one, including the police, had any idea why Tolbert would have been the victim of what appeared to be a professional killing.

A toxicological report came back showing no trace of drugs in the victim's blood.

A tip line had been set up for information, but nothing credible had come in during the first forty-eight hours, obviously the critical time in any murder investigation.

The police would work the case, but with no clues to go on and no tips to check out, the chance that they would solve it was very small.

Dr. Dowling is nervous.

I know that because when he gets in my car, he says, "I'm nervous."

He's not used to dealing with the police, and certainly and fortunately has had no previous experience with any murder investigation.

"Nothing to worry about," I say. "Just tell Pete what you know and then you're done with it. You're not a central player here."

"I reconfirmed with Debra that there is no chance the guy who dropped Truman off was twenty years old. Which reminds me, what are we going to do about Truman?"

"Don't worry, I'll deal with it and take care of him. He'll be fine."

We arrive at the station house and go in. The desk sergeant unsuccessfully tries to stifle a moan when he sees me; we go back a ways, and while he hates all defense attorneys, I suspect he envisions me in a special kind of hell.

"You turning yourself in?" he asks.

"Why?" I ask. "You hoping to strip search me?" Then, "We're here to see Pete; known as Captain Stanton to ass lickers such as yourself."

He starts to retort, thinks better of it, and then calls Pete to tell him we're here. When he gets off the phone, he just moves his head in the direction of Pete's office, which is his way of telling me we can go.

Before we do, I say, "Black. No sugar. And a Diet Coke for my friend. Get a move on, we're thirsty."

We go back to Pete's office, and when we arrive, he says, "My day is complete."

"Pete, this is Dr. Dowling. He's a professional person, still another example of what you could have become if you had gotten past the seventh grade."

He just frowns and shakes hands with Dowling. "What kind of doctor are you?"

"A veterinarian."

Pete nods. "Why am I not surprised?" Then, "Let's hear what you have to say."

I give Dowling the floor and he tells the story in pretty much the same manner he told it to me. The only change is that he underplays his obligation to put Truman down once the alleged owner paid the money for it.

Pete listens to the story and says, "Let me have the guy's name."

"It's a fake," I say. "We checked."

"Maybe we can do a more detailed check."

"The name he gave was Charlie Henderson; he gave a fake address and phone number."

"No license plate number?"

Dowling shakes his head. "No. My receptionist would have had no reason to look."

"Okay. Thanks for coming in."

"What do you think, Sherlock?" I ask.

"I think Haley was killed, his dog ran off, and this guy found him."

I nod. "So he found the dog, but instead of taking him to the pound or just ignoring him and letting him run stray, he decided to take the dog to a vet, use fake names for himself and the dog, and then pay to have him killed?" I turn to Dowling. "How much did he pay?"

"One hundred ninety-five dollars. In cash."

I nod and turn to Pete. "That makes sense to you? By that I mean, can you imagine a single human being on the planet behaving that way?"

"Maybe he took the dog into his house and it bit him, or his kid. So he wanted to make sure the dog couldn't bite anyone else. Who knows? This is a homicide case; I think they handle dog-napping down the hall."

Pete clearly wants nothing to do with this, so Dowling and I stand to leave. Before we do, Pete asks, "Where's the dog now?"

"You mean my client?" I ask. "He's in my protective custody."

"He's evidence in the case," Pete says.

"We're willing to come in and talk anytime. In the meantime, I'll send a copy of his paw prints to forensics."

27

Our son, Ricky, is at summer camp in upstate New York.

He left two weeks ago, and Laurie bought him enough camp clothing that if they suddenly decide the summer is going to be extended from eight weeks to four years, he will still never have to wear the same outfit twice. Knowing Ricky as I do, when he comes home, 80 percent of the stuff will still have the tags on.

Laurie says we should both write to him every day, but after three days my conversational well ran dry. Most of my letters now are made up of questions. "How's camp?" "You playing sports?" You enjoying yourself?" "How's the food?"

His answers are incredibly revealing. "Good." "Yes." "Yes." "Okay." I think Ricky is as bored with the whole letter-writing thing as I am.

But I have to admit that I am amazed at

how much I miss him. Ricky is ten; we adopted him when he was eight. In all that time, I don't think more than a day or two has gone by without me seeing him, and his absence really makes the house seem empty.

One other effect that his departure has had is that Laurie and I don't have to be guarded in our conversation when it comes to talking about a case. We always make an effort not to discuss things like murders in front of him, although I think he unfortunately picks up quite a bit of it anyway.

Right now Laurie and I are having breakfast, and I've just asked, "Why is this bothering me?" I'm talking about the situation with Truman and Pete's dismissal of him as a factor in the case.

She thinks for a moment. "It's possible — and I'm just brain-storming here — that you might be a human being with human emotions."

"Come on, let's be serious."

"I mean it, Andy. Your mind, which is a bit warped but always logical, realizes that the situation doesn't seem to make sense. And you know that to just let it drop, with someone sitting in jail on a murder charge, would be the wrong thing to do."

"You think my mind is warped?"

"Only in the sense that it is abnormal,

twisted, and slightly bent."

I nod. "Oh, sure, when you put it that way . . . So what should I do?" I regret the question the moment I ask it, because I know what the answer is going to be.

"Look into it; see what you can find out," she says, validating my prediction. "You can do it without becoming too involved. Then when you learn whatever it is you learn, you can decide on your next steps. I'll even help you."

"Okay. But you need to understand one thing: I'm not doing it as a lawyer. I'm doing it as a private citizen."

"You are a private citizen," she says.

"Exactly. You obviously understand. Where should we start?"

"With the victim."

I am constantly surprised, even though no one else is, by the amount of information that is available online. You can find out anything about anyone or anything at any time. I have no idea who puts it all out there, or why they do, but it's there.

Of course, even when it comes to computer searches, there are different levels and abilities. On a scale of one to ten, with ten being the highest and best, I'm a one. On a scale of one to fifty, with fifty being the highest and best, I'm still a one.

If Ricky were home, I could turn to him. Even at his young age, he has already forgotten more about computers and technology than I will ever know about them. But since we don't like to talk murders in front of him, I tend to shy away from having him research them.

I could also just ask Laurie, who sits somewhere between Ricky and me in the tech-savvy rankings.

But instead I call Sam Willis. Sam is my accountant, but that is just his day job. He is also my computer guy, possessing all the skills necessary to perform the legal and other-than-legal work my practice often requires.

Simply put, Sam is a genius hacker, capable of accessing anything, anywhere. This task is beneath him; it's like asking Messi or Ronaldo to play a game of kick the can.

But when I ask him for the rundown on the deceased Mr. Haley, he seems anxious to help. Sam loves when I take cases almost as much as I hate taking them, so we balance each other out.

"Sam, while you're at it, see what you can find out about Joey Gamble. He's been arrested for the crime; you can probably find out his address from newspaper accounts."

"You got it, Chief."

" 'Chief'? Sam, you're not a cop. You're an accountant. It's why you carry a pencil instead of a gun."

"Don't kill the dream, Andy. Don't kill the dream."

Once I've sent Sam on his mission, I head down to Dr. Dowling's to pick up Truman. I've convinced Dr. Dowling that he is not breaking the law by letting Truman live, though I doubt that he would have had the heart to put down a healthy, innocent dog anyway.

As I'm leaving, he once again asks me to confirm that this is okay.

"The guy signed a contract with you using a fake name, so there is no legally binding contract."

"He paid for it."

"So donate the money to the Humane Society. Trust me on this."

He does trust me, so I leave with Truman and take him down to the Tara Foundation. Willie is out, but his wife, Sondra, is watching over things. Both of them are incredibly dedicated.

"He's adorable, Andy," she says, a sentiment which I share. "How long will he be with us?"

"Hard to say, but best not to place him

until his ownership issue is fully resolved."

She nods. "Okay. We'll see to it that he has a bunch of friends to play with."

I nod. "Good; he's been through a rough time. Give him anything he wants; put it on my tab."

The setting was a little weird, which by this point was to be expected.

As George Adams pulled up, he saw what was obviously an abandoned playground. A swing set, a seesaw, and some other equipment that had obviously not been used in a very long time sat in the weeds, rusting and rotting.

Some people might have taken a moment to reflect on the scene, possibly realizing, maybe with some sadness, that at one point this setting would have been filled with the laughter of small children under the watchful eyes of their doting parents.

Those people were not George Adams.

George didn't like kids; he never had. One of the things George didn't like about them was that they grew up to be adults, and George didn't like adults either. George was not a particularly sociable person.

Probably the main reason George had gotten married for a second time was that the new wife, Denise, didn't want kids either. It had been one of the reasons George dumped his previous wife; she had claimed not to be fulfilled without a little brat running around. Let her go fulfill herself somewhere else.

But Denise did like dogs, and even though George didn't, he was going to go along with it. Because he loved Denise.

It turned out to be a big mistake.

There was a small stand that looked like at one point it had sold ice cream, or popcorn, or whatever the hell else little kids forced their parents to buy. But now it looked weather-beaten and about to fall over.

That's where George walked to, because that's where the guy who wanted to be called Mister said they would meet. George knew that his name was Frank Silvio; Tony Longo had found that out long ago, and then George had checked Silvio out.

But if Silvio wanted to be called Mister, George didn't care one way or the other. He would call him whatever the hell he wanted. That was for the same reason that he didn't mind waiting for Silvio even though he was late to show up at the playground.

Whatever Silvio did was fine, because Silvio was bringing the money.

It was only the second half of the money; the first fifty thousand had been paid in advance. George thought back to the day he had first been approached by Silvio. It was at a McDonald's in Haddonfield; he was eating alone when Silvio sat down in his booth and put a thousand dollars in hundreds on the table.

He told George that if he wanted to talk about getting much more, he'd be waiting in his car outside. If not, George could just use the money to buy about five hundred Big Macs.

George hadn't agonized over the decision; he almost beat Silvio to his car. And Silvio didn't beat around the bush; he started by saying he had an offer to make, which he had already cleared with George's boss, Fat Tony Longo.

Silvio had obviously done research on George and knew he was an enforcer for Longo in the Philly area. And he knew that for a hundred grand in cash, fifty of it up front, George wouldn't hesitate to commit a murder.

Hell, he'd have done it for half that.

George had only been at the playground for ten minutes when Silvio pulled up. He was carrying a briefcase; it looked like the same make and model that had contained the first fifty grand.

As was obviously his style, Silvio came right to the point. "Tell me everything."

George shrugged, a combination of nonchalance and obvious pride. "Nothing to tell. I came in through the back door, picked the lock in no time. One shot in the back, another in the head to make sure. Then I took the items and threw open some drawers to make it look like the place had been gone through. Then I took some of the other things. Just like we talked about."

"Where is it?"

"You mean the computer and the video stuff?"

Silvio nodded. "That's what I mean."

"It's in my car. And I got that card out of the camera also."

"Good. So there were no problems?" Silvio asked.

"Nah. He never knew what hit him. I went out the way I came in."

"What about the dog?"

George just about did a double take. "How did you know about that?"

"What about the dog?" The tone in Silvio's voice made it obvious that he was doing the questioning, not the answering.

"The guy had a dog; I think one of those bulldogs. My wife wants one of them, so I grabbed it. I got it back to the apartment and in the morning the piece of garbage bit me on the hand. So I had him killed."

"You killed him?"

"Nah, I took him to a vet." The irony is that George, having just killed the dog's owner, never considered killing the dog himself. "I used a fake name and the dog didn't have a tag or collar or anything. No way to trace him."

Silvio already had all this information; he just wanted to see what George would say. He also knew things George didn't know. He knew that George's wife, Denise, had already been killed, and the fifty grand advance had been recovered from George's house. And he knew that George was soon going to follow Denise to the great beyond.

And just like the guy George had killed, George never knew what hit him.

James Haley was not Steven Spielberg.

I know this because included in Sam's comprehensive online rundown on Haley is a trailer for his upcoming documentary, *The World Below,* which was shot on the west coast of Florida.

Actually, it looks like the film is more about getting to that "world below"; it's an examination of scuba and sponge diving. Based on the trailer, which is only about ninety seconds long, the documentary doesn't seem to have a point of view on the sport (if scuba diving is, in fact, a sport), but rather promises to present its good and bad aspects.

I've never understood diving, though I admit that could be because I've never tried it. That lack of understanding is not likely to change, because if there is one thing in this world that I am certain of, it is that I am never going to try it.

If I were to go to a Caribbean beach resort, which I almost never do, I would have two basic options. One would be to lie under an umbrella by the pool, reading and sipping piña coladas. When I tired of that, I could amble into the casino, play some blackjack, and sip more piña coladas.

Or I could dive into eighty feet of water, which is about seventy-four feet taller than I am, standing on my toes. I could stick a large plastic thing in my mouth and place what looks like a two-ton tank on my back when I jump into the ocean. Heavy things like that are what mobsters put on bodies to make sure they don't come to the surface.

Then, once submerged in all that water, and assuming I could still breathe, I could hope that the pressure does not cause my eyeballs to explode. Then I could be on the lookout for all kinds of sharks and other killer fish. Even normal fish give me the creeps; if I order one in a restaurant, I make them fillet it and remove the head before bringing it to me. If they don't, I can feel the eyes staring at me, and I know the fish is thinking, *You win this round, pal, but when you go scuba diving, your ass is mine. That's my turf.*

All this time I could hope that the guy who filled the tanks didn't skimp on the air and instead filled them to the top, because if he didn't, I could find myself sucking on whatever is the opposite of air.

The trailer spends at least half its time on sponge diving, which is different in that the thing in the diver's mouth is attached by a hose to a pump on a boat. He also wears a full bodysuit and a metal helmet, which makes him look like the Creature from the Something Lagoon.

All of this means that the mouth thing, the suit, the hose, and the pump all have to be working flawlessly in order for the diver to continue breathing.

I have never in my life owned a device that always worked flawlessly, and in this case I would be counting on four? I don't think so.

Of course, if I was the amateur diver, I probably would not know the person driving the boat, since we might have just met. For all I know, he could be totally nuts and might start racing the boat all over the place, thereby dragging me along by my teeth.

And if everything worked great, the upside is that I'd wind up with a free sponge? I believe there are easier ways to get sponges, at reasonable cost, with no chance of dying.

All in all, the bottom of the ocean is, to

me, a world that would gradually turn into a nightmare. I can imagine myself suffocating and starting to panic as I came to the realization that escaping this foreign place was impossible. The only similar experience I have ever had was when Laurie took me to an IKEA.

The documentary footage seems for the most part unremarkable. It points out the dangers of unscrupulous and untrained instructors, looking to make a quick buck off of unsuspecting newcomers to the sport. But it also speaks to the beauty of the undersea world and the uniqueness of the experience.

According to Sam, the actual film when completed will be available on video but will never have a theatrical run. Of course, now that the filmmaker is dead, I would imagine the finishing of the film and its release are somewhat up in the air, or underwater.

Sam provided me with another video, a finished project that Haley seems to have shot a couple of years ago. It's another documentary, this one about a California town that has literally run out of well water. The people living there woke up one morning and turned on their taps, and nothing happened.

The film is about how they are coping with a dry life while hoping for the end of the drought. It's interesting, but obviously depressing.

Having seen enough video, I turn to the biographical information Sam has provided. Haley grew up in Toledo, Ohio, and moved around some before settling back there. He has a brother in Oregon, but was never married and had no children.

Haley went to the University of Maine in Orono and then joined the army. He reached the rank of captain and served twelve years. He continued to serve in the Army Reserve and was called up twice for tours in Afghanistan and Iraq.

Sam has also taken a semi-intrusive, not completely legal online look at Haley's recent life. There is really nothing unusual to see; no arrests, not much debt, no alarming financial information. Sam also mentions that Paterson was apparently not going to be the only city featured in the "urban blight" film. Haley had been using a car that he rented when he landed at Newark Airport, and he was set to return it in Washington, D.C., next week.

There is nothing in here that would give me the slightest indication as to why James Haley was murdered or who murdered him.

And certainly there is no clue as to how his dog wound up barely avoiding a death sentence at a Glen Rock, New Jersey, veterinarian's office.

My work ethic tells me to forget about the whole thing, but there are two problems with that. One is that I really would like to find out who would be so anxious to put down an innocent dog like Truman. Getting revenge on that person might be nice.

The other reason I can't drop it is that Laurie would stare at me disapprovingly. I have been on the receiving end of those kinds of stares from her before, and it is no fun, no fun at all. Think Mike Tyson glaring at his opponent while getting instructions from the referee before a fight.

For the moment, at least, there's nothing more to learn about the victim. Since I have no idea who the guy was who dropped Truman at the vet, and since I have already thoroughly interrogated Truman, the only other avenue open to me is to learn about the accused.

Which means I will once again have to watch a touchdown.

Billy "Bulldog" Cameron's life was changed by the advent of the smartphone.

Now instead of only verbally informing every single person he meets that he caught the touchdown pass that enabled Georgia to beat Auburn twenty-five years ago, he can actually show them the play, right there on his phone.

I am one of the more receptive viewers, even though by now I've probably seen the play ten times. That's because I am a football fan and I secretly wish I had caught a touchdown pass in college. Of course, I would also have liked to have thrown one, or pitched a shutout, or hit a three-pointer, but alas, none of those was meant to be.

My school, NYU, didn't even have a football team. That's probably just as well, since the nickname for NYU's sports teams is actually "the Violets." I kid you not.

You think that might make football recruiting difficult? You think Bronko Nagurski, Jim Brown, Dick Butkus, and Lawrence Taylor secretly longed to be known as "Violets"?

"Gonna be a tough game today, guys . . . better buckle up those chinstraps. We're playing the Violets."

The game in which Billy caught the pass was not particularly meaningful; all it did was guarantee Georgia third place in the SEC that year. But that doesn't stop Billy from bragging about it.

So Billy's immodesty is the bad news; the good news is that he has devoted his entire adult life and professional career to helping people. He runs the Public Defender's Office, which is a sure way for a lawyer to be overworked and underpaid.

For that reason, when I arrive at Billy's office, I let him show me the video yet again, and I marvel at the move that he put on the hapless Auburn defensive back. Billy points out, as he does every time, that the defensive back subsequently played for the Oakland Raiders for six games.

He finally clicks off the phone and says, "What can I do for you, Andy?"

"Tell me about Joey Gamble."

"You want to take the case?"

"Not a chance." Billy would like nothing

better than for me to represent Joey; he doesn't have nearly enough lawyers to go around.

"Then why the interest?"

There's no reason that any of this should be a secret, so I tell him all about Dr. Dowling and Truman.

"Interesting," he says.

"Wow. You public defender guys are sharp as tacks."

He laughs. Then, "So, you want to know about Joey Gamble? He's a good kid. I actually know him; I coached him in basketball when he was twelve and I was helping out in the Big Brother program."

This guy is amazing. "You're a public defender and a Big Brother?"

He nods and smiles. "And did I mention I caught a touchdown pass against Auburn?"

"I believe I heard that somewhere. So could Gamble have done this?"

He shrugs. "I would hope not, but you never know. He got in with some bad kids a couple of years ago and was arrested a couple of times for petty theft. Nothing too serious, and the charges were dropped, but still not a good sign. Then I heard he'd reformed; his grandmother is a great lady, and she read him the riot act. Now this."

"Do they have evidence?"

He nods. "They do."

"Can I see the file?"

He nods. "I'll have a copy made, which means for the moment you're one of his lawyers. Okay? You can bail out at any time."

"Sure." The only way Billy can give me the file is to technically have me on the case. That's no problem.

Billy calls his assistant to have the copy made. "Maybe when you read it, you'll want to take it over."

"Maybe the sun won't come up tomorrow. I've only taken it this far because Laurie has this weird thing about disliking injustice."

He laughs. "What the hell is she doing with you?"

"Billy, I ask myself that every day."

It takes about ten minutes for the copy of the file to be made, so Billy uses the time to describe further details of his game-winning catch against Auburn. As I'm finally getting up to leave, his phone rings. After answering it, he hands it to me. "It's Laurie."

I'm not worried; she knew I was here, and I've had my cell phone turned off during the meeting. That lack of worry lasts until she says, "Andy, meet me at Dr. Dowling's."

"Are Tara and Sebastian okay?"

"They're fine. It's about the situation with

Truman. We think we know who dropped him off."

"Who?"

"Just meet me there and I'll show you."

49

This time Dr. Dowling's office is a bit more crowded.

Truman isn't here, but Laurie is, along with Dowling and Debra, his receptionist. It was Debra who dealt with the guy who brought Truman in to be euthanized. Right now she's looking very upset; my guess is that she had not expected the receptionist job to be quite this stressful.

In fact, no one in the room looks particularly happy. I've got a feeling I'm about to join that club. "What's going on?" I ask reluctantly.

"Take a look at this," Laurie says, and she walks around behind Dowling, who is sitting at his desk. I go there as well, because clearly the answer is on his computer.

He tilts the monitor so I can read what is there. It's a news story in the *Philadelphia Inquirer* about the murder of a woman in her house in suburban Philly. As I read, I see that the deceased's name is Denise Adams, and that she was the wife of George Adams, who seems to be a man of less-than-flawless reputation.

George has been in prison on three different occasions, assault with a deadly weapon being the most serious of the crimes he's been convicted of. He is said to have been gainfully employed by an organized crime enterprise in Philadelphia. He is also apparently nowhere to be found, all of which makes him a logical suspect in his wife's brutal murder.

"This is the guy?" I ask Debra, pointing at his photo.

She nods. "I'm sure of it."

"The story made the local news here," Laurie says, "because Adams was apparently spotted in this area. That's where Debra saw it."

I read through the article again to see when the woman's murder took place. It was about thirty-six hours after Truman was dropped off.

"Am I going to have to talk to the police?" Debra asks, clearly nervous at the prospect.

I'd like to tell her she shouldn't talk to anyone at this point because I want to take more time to investigate and figure out what might be going on. But this guy Adams is wanted for murder, and if Debra has information about that, she is under an obvious obligation to report it.

So I nod. "Yes, but for now, here's what I think you should do. There's a tip line mentioned in that article. Call it and say that you think you saw the man they're looking for. They'll take down the information and say that they will be contacting you. That will likely take a while, and by then we should know quite a bit more."

"Will you be there when they talk to me?"

"If you want me to, of course."

"I want you to," she says.

Debra asks us to stay while she calls the tip line, and we do. If it's like every other tip line on a case that gets a lot of publicity, the police will be inundated with calls. They will try to narrow down the contacts that seem worthy of follow-up, and then prioritize those with their limited manpower for callback.

To put it another way, Debra does not need to sit by the phone.

Laurie and I leave, going home in our separate cars. Once we're both in the house, I sit in the den and Laurie comes in with a couple of glasses of wine. A dreaded "talk" seems to be imminent.

We both sit on the couch. "Don't say it," I say.

She nods. "Fine."

What follows is about thirty seconds of silence, which feels like a year. Finally, and inevitably, I break. "Okay, say it."

She nods. "Two murders are committed very close together in time, one near Philadelphia and one here. The man suspected in one murder turns up with the second victim's dog, under circumstances that give new meaning to the word *suspicious.* How am I doing so far?"

"Seems pretty accurate."

She smiles. "Good. Another person, who is not the aforementioned man, sits in jail accused of the second murder. There would seem to be a reasonable question as to his guilt, pending further information."

"I have his file to read," I say.

"Good. Once you do, if the file fails to address the curious circumstances that I've laid out, I would describe you as uniquely qualified to get to the bottom of all of this."

"Why me?" I ask.

"Because it's what you do, and you do it better than just about anyone else. And because I've noticed you have some free time on your hands."

"Free time? I have to write a letter to

Ricky, I need to get a haircut, and I simply must buy some new socks. My plate is full."

"Andy . . ."

"I'll read the file."

The file that Billy gave me on the Haley murder is a lot thinner than it's going to be.

The case has really just begun; there will be much more evidence to process and many more people to interview. Of course, the fact that the police have already made an arrest, despite the early stage of the investigation, can easily be interpreted as a sign of the confidence law enforcement has that Joey Gamble is the killer.

Defense lawyers like myself love to argue the "rush to judgment" theory; we claim that had the cops simply not focused on our client and kept investigating, they would have come upon the real guilty party. While there are rare occasions when we're right, the truth is that police and prosecutors don't like to be caught making mistakes. Which means they don't want to hurriedly arrest the wrong person and have it come back to bite them in the ass.

In this case, it's obvious why they are so confident. Joey Gamble's fingerprints are all over Haley's house, or at least in the living room, kitchen, and bathroom. In addition, he was seen leaving the house through the front door by a neighbor around the time that the coroner estimated Haley's death occurred. A different neighbor, who had seen Haley's body through the back door, had made the 911 call that brought the police to the scene.

Gamble was interviewed by the police after he foolishly consented to talk without a lawyer present. He told them he was there to be interviewed by Haley for a film he was making, and that Haley was alive and well when he left.

The house had been ransacked as well, though it is impossible to know what was taken, since the police have no way of knowing what was there in the first place.

DNA tests are in the process of being done, but there is little doubt that they will confirm Gamble's presence at the house. It is pretty much impossible to spend time in a room and leave a bunch of fingerprints, but not leave DNA.

Prosecutors do not have to prove motive, and there is no specific mention of motive in this file, but it's clear that the police theory is that this was a robbery gone bad.

There is also no mention of Truman. I would think that if the neighbor had seen Gamble leaving with a dog, it would have made it into his witness report. But he didn't, and the police report does not speak to the issue at all. That basically makes sense, since it wouldn't have seemed particularly important to them one way or the other.

When I'm done going through the file, a process which takes maybe forty-five minutes, I tell Laurie the basics. Her first question is a good one. "Does the witness say if Gamble left the front door open behind him?"

I shake my head. "Doesn't mention it. I would assume if he had, it's something that the witness would have noticed."

"So Truman couldn't have run off."

"So it seems, unless he went out the back door."

"But ultimately he wound up with George Adams, who in turn decided to pay to have him killed."

"It's possible that Debra could be wrong in her identification; she's pretty shaken by everything."

Laurie nods. "Possible, but we know for sure that someone other than Joey Gamble wound up with Truman and brought him to Dowling's office. And in doing so, that person acted in a way that seems to defy logic."

"Very true."

"So what do we do now?" she asks.

"Now we forget about the whole thing and hope it ends happily for everyone?"

"Try again."

"Now I tell Billy what we know, so he can relay it to the public defender he's assigned to Gamble's case?"

"Closer, but still wrong," she says.

"We continue to investigate so we can convince ourselves that justice is really going to be served?"

"Bingo."

I frown. "You're becoming very predictable."

She smiles. "It's part of my charm."

I need to speak to Pete Stanton again.

It's not something I'm looking forward to, but there is an obligation to tell him that Debra believes she has seen and spoken to George Adams, wanted for the murder of his wife down in Philadelphia.

Rather than go to Pete's office, I'm going to talk to him tonight at Charlie's. Everything, even unproductive conversations, goes down better with burgers, fries, beer, and sports.

Laurie and I have an early dinner. Much as I miss Ricky, there is a positive to him being away at camp and not at these dinners. With him home, dinners at our house had an unpleasant additional aspect.

Vegetables.

I don't eat vegetables, with the notable exceptions of corn and cucumbers. Laurie has never met a vegetable she didn't like; she's like a great-looking human rabbit.

Ricky saw and analyzed this tug of war and came out on my side, which is to say, he is firmly in my anti-vegetable camp. While I was flattered and humbled by the support, even I recognize that this is an unhealthy way for a growing boy to eat. For that reason, I agreed to suck it up and eat that green garbage, so as to get him to do the same.

Tonight we are having salmon, which is barely tolerable by itself, and Laurie has a side of peas. In the world of disgusting vegetables, peas occupy a position at the top of the revolting heap. The taste is bad enough, but the consistency of the little round pellets takes them to a far worse level. Peas actually make salmon look good; peas would make horse manure look good.

Last time we had them, Ricky was home, and he asked, with some measure of horror, "You gonna eat those, Dad?"

I nodded. "Mmmm, boy. You betcha." With that, I put a spoonful of the loathsome things into my mouth. It wasn't easy; I could barely force myself to part my lips.

Ricky watched me as I ate. What I didn't let him see was my technique. I put the peas in my mouth but didn't chew them, instead swallowing them as if they were aspirin. Then, once they had cleared my mouth and taste buds, I pretended to chew. It was still awful, but preferable to biting into them.

Laurie had trouble concealing a smile at my discomfort. She was and is happy that Ricky and I are both eating this healthy crap, and she liked and appreciated that I was willing to do it.

What I did for love . . . kiss today good-bye and point me toward tomorrow.

Once we're finished, I head down to Charlie's; four or five hundred crisp french fries should be enough to get the taste of healthy salmon out of my mouth, especially when they're washed down with beer.

Pete and Vince are at our usual table when I get there, which is not exactly a big surprise. I think Vince actually has his ass stapled to the chair, because when he turns to watch different televisions showing different games, the chair seems to turn with him.

Mostly we're watching the Mets game, and after the third inning, I say to Pete, "We have more business to discuss."

He barely stifles a moan. "What happened? Did the victim's pet canary fly into your window?"

I turn to Vince. "Here's your choice. A: You can go sit over there for the duration of this conversation, or B: you can agree that it's off the record."

"Off the record?" he asks. "I'm not familiar with that phrase. Is there a third option?"

I nod. "Yes. Pete and I can have the talk in his office tomorrow, and you can pay for your own food and beer for the rest of your natural life."

"Let's go with B," he says.

"Off the record?"

"Way off," he says. "Totally off."

"Good. It's a treat to meet a man of principle." With that I turn to Pete and inform him of Debra identifying George Adams as the man who brought Truman in. "He's the guy wanted for the murder of his wife in Philadelphia."

"This is the same receptionist who supplied the information on the Haley murder?"

"Yes. Obviously."

"Anything else she want to report on? Maybe the Kennedy assassination? Or did she run into John Wilkes Booth in the supermarket?"

"Pete, as her attorney, this conversation represents her officially reporting what she knows to the proper authorities, although referring to you as a 'proper authority' is an insult to proper authorities everywhere. In any event, you can do whatever you want with it. Just so you know, she also called the Philly tip line."

"You and your client are model citizens. I'll alert the Philly cops; I'm sure you'll hear from them."

"You know, if this guy could murder his wife down there, he could also have murdered someone up here, say, on Thirty-ninth Street."

"Except the guy who really did it is in jail."

"If you arrested him, the chance that he's actually guilty is close to absolute zero."

"You've got time on your hands," he says. "Why don't you prove it?"

"I'm afraid I might have to," I say, because I really am afraid I might have to at least try.

Vince finally speaks. "I forget, was this on or off the record?"

Laurie spent most of her career as a Paterson cop; she rose to the rank of lieutenant.

The fact that she was so well liked, and retains so many friends on the force, is probably the only reason the current Paterson cops haven't put a hit out on me. As a defense attorney, I am widely and naturally disliked by law enforcement. As a thoroughly obnoxious defense attorney, that dislike reaches rare heights.

In addition to keeping me alive, Laurie's law enforcement relationships sometimes help in other ways, and today is another example. She once worked in concert with the Philadelphia Police Department on a case in which a suspect in a murder case had fled there. Laurie had gone down to question the guy, and ultimately to extradite him.

She worked with Sergeant Jack Rubin, and they have maintained a Christmas/birthday card relationship ever since. We took Jack and his wife out to dinner once when they spent a few days in New York, and I was on my best behavior.

So I'm calling Jack to see what he knows about George Adams and the murder of Adams's wife. I'm not sure that her murder has anything at all to do with Truman or the murder of James Haley, but my approach is usually to gather as much information as I can and put off worrying about whether it is valuable or relevant until later.

This is the way I usually operate on a case, the only difference now being that I'm not really involved in this one. For example, by now I would have extensively interviewed and debriefed my client, something I haven't done, since I don't actually have a client.

I said I was calling Sergeant Rubin, but that is not actually the case. Laurie is calling him and will then put me on the phone. We do it like this because Laurie has certain important qualities that I lack, such as likeability, warmth, and general humanity. It has a tendency to soften people up so that they find me more tolerable.

This time the softening-up takes about ten minutes, and then she hands me the phone. I chitchat with Rubin for almost ten seconds and then ask him what he knows about George Adams.

"This about the two killings down here?"

"What two killings?" I ask.

"We've got a possible serial killer in the making. Homeless men are turning up dead. They're being shot in the head, executed."

"Why would you think I'd be asking about that?"

"Because you just had a similar murder up there. Clifton is near Paterson, right?"

"Yes, but I haven't heard about it."

"You sure you're a criminal defense attorney?"

"I have my doubts, and proud of it," I say. "And I make sure not to watch the news. Is Adams a suspect in those two murders?"

"Not yet, but you never know. He's a piece of garbage," Jack says. "No brains, no conscience, no fear. Which makes him valuable to the people who control him."

"Who controls him?"

"Mostly Fat Tony Longo."

"Fat Tony Longo?"

"Yeah," Jack says. "They call him that because his name is Tony Longo and he's fat."

"He sounds like a heck of a guy. I assume Fat Tony doesn't run a philanthropic organization?"

"You assume correctly. But the word on the street is that Fat Tony claims to have no idea where George is, or what the hell he is up to. Of course, the word on the street is rarely correct."

"Why did George kill his wife?"

"Who says he did?"

"The media."

"That's where you get your information? It's true — we're looking for George, although it's not my case. But if you're asking me, which I assume you are, I don't think he did it."

"Why not?"

"Well, first of all, people who know George have always been amazed at how Denise had him wrapped around her little finger. But that's not the real reason. He could always have snapped; George has spent his entire life in pre-snap mode."

"And the real reason?"

"It's not his style; it's not how George would have done it. He wouldn't have left her body there; he would have hidden it where no one could find it and gone on with his life. If anyone asked, he would claim she went to live with her long-lost sister."

I tell him about the Haley murder and George winding up with Truman. "Doesn't sound like George either," he says. "I would think he would just put a bullet in the dog's head."

I understand what Jack is saying, but it doesn't clear anything up. Why and how did Adams wind up with Truman in the first place? Why not just let him run stray? Why not kill the dog himself if he wanted him dead? These are questions Jack would have no idea how to answer.

"So, bottom line, what do you think?" I ask.

He pauses for a few moments, weighing his words. "I think it's possible that the lady at the vet office is wrong in thinking it was George."

"And if she's right?"

"I'll say this. If George had any connection whatsoever to a murder, and this dog would represent a connection, then George is somehow involved in that murder. It doesn't mean the guy they arrested is innocent, but George is not just a bystander. There aren't coincidences that big."

I've got a big decision to make.

I've been hovering around the periphery of the Haley murder case, gathering information but not taking anything approaching an active role. I have no personal involvement yet, beyond a willingness to help Dr. Dowling.

But he doesn't really need my help any longer, so it's time to decide whether to take the key step. There's no escaping the obvious . . . if I'm going to make the next logical move in looking into this case, I need to talk to the accused.

If I do that, it creates the danger of this becoming personal. God forbid I should like the kid, or think it's credible that he's innocent. Then I will really be stuck.

But there's another aspect to this that's even worse. There's a guy out there, George Adams, who may have killed his wife. I can't be sure of that; in fact, Sergeant Jack Rubin has his doubts. But even he believes Adams is a murderer; that's part of Adams's résumé.

And no matter what Adams has done or not done to various people, Adams is guilty of the attempted murder of Truman. I'm certain of that, just as I'm certain that I can't simply let him get away with it.

I share all of this with Laurie, and her response is, "You want me to go with you?"

"Where?"

"To the jail to talk to Joey Gamble."

"I haven't decided to do that yet."

"Of course you have," she says.

"I'd need to talk to Bulldog and set it up. His people are handling the case."

She nods. "I already took care of that. He was thrilled and has already notified the jail personnel. You're good to go."

"So, is it that you think you know me, or that you think you can control me?" I ask.

"You're an independent man, Andy. No one can control you."

"You're controlling me now."

She nods. "What tipped you off?" Then, "So do you want me to go to the jail with you?"

"No, I'm an independent, uncontrollable man."

I take my independence and head down

to the jail by myself to see Joey Gamble. It's not the quickest and easiest thing to do. As a designated lawyer, I have the right to visit and talk to Gamble in private, but as people who dislike lawyers, the jail personnel have the right to take their sweet time about making it happen.

When Joey is finally brought in, his appearance surprises me. I'm not talking about the fear in his eyes and face; that is to be expected. He's had a few run-ins with the law before, but nothing like this. This is a murder charge that he's facing; it is fair to say that if he is convicted, any meaningful life he might lead is over.

What surprises me about him is his size. He can't be more than five foot seven, a hundred and forty pounds. I've got him by three inches and twenty-five pounds, and nobody has ever worried about running into me in a dark alley.

He eyes me suspiciously. "Who are you?"

"My name is Andy Carpenter. I'm a lawyer."

"My lawyer?"

"Not exactly."

"So whose side are you on?" he asks, a perfectly reasonable question.

"Either yours or nobody's," I say, and then explain that I'm helping the Public Defender's Office at this point. Whether I become involved in the case is still to be determined.

He looks like he doesn't fully understand, but finally shrugs and says, "Okay, what do you want?" He's already exhausted by the process, and the fear, and the worry. At some point he'll become partially numb to it, but that's a ways off.

"I want to know why your fingerprints are all over James Haley's apartment."

"Because I was in there."

At least he's not claiming otherwise; denying clear forensic evidence is a nonstarter. "Why were you in there?"

"He wanted to ask me questions," Gamble says. "He had been in the neighborhood, filming stuff, and he wanted me to be in his movie. To talk to him about what it was like in the neighborhood."

"Why you?"

Gamble shrugs. "I don't know. I was interested in what he was doing, and I was asking questions about it. Everybody else seemed pissed off that he was there. So maybe he thought I'd be willing to talk."

"Why was everybody else pissed off?"

He shrugs again. " 'Cause he wasn't from the neighborhood, you know? What goes on there wasn't his business, at least that's what people thought."

"So you went to his place and talked to him. What about?"

"First he was asking general stuff, like was it hard to find work, and did people ever leave, and did I go to school . . . that kind of stuff. So I answered him, but I don't think he cared much."

"Why do you say that?"

He shrugs. "Just a feeling I had. I'm used to people not giving a shit what I say."

"Were you being filmed during this time?"

He nods. "Yes — at least he said so. The camera seemed to be on."

"You said 'at first' he was asking general stuff. That changed?"

"He started asking me about drug stuff, whether a lot of guys were users, what kind of drugs, things like that. I told him I didn't know anything about it, and then he asked about . . ." He hesitates before finishing the sentence. "About Chico Simmons."

"Who is Chico Simmons?" He looks at me like I would look at someone who'd just asked "Who is LeBron James?"

"He's an important guy in the neighborhood."

"A gang leader?"

He frowns. "He's got people," is his grudging response. "He's got a lot of people."

"Are you one of them?"

"No."

"So what did you tell him about Chico Simmons?"

He laughs a short laugh. "Nothing. Are you crazy?"

"What did he want to know?"

"I don't know. I told him I never heard of Chico. I figure he knew I was lying and wasn't going to tell him anything, so that was pretty much it. He turned off the camera and said we were done."

"So you left at what time?"

"I think it was about eight thirty."

I know that the coroner placed the time of death as between eight and ten, so Gamble's timeline is not helpful. "Did you leave through the front door or the back?"

"The front."

"Did you see anybody around?"

"Not that I remember." Then, "Maybe a neighbor. A guy."

"Did Haley have a dog?" I ask.

"Yeah. He was sitting on a couch the whole time we talked, like he was listening in."

"What was the dog's name?"

"How the hell should I know?"

I show him a photograph of Truman. "Does this look like the dog?"

He nods. "Yeah, could be. I think so, yeah."

I next take out a photo of George Adams that we printed off the internet. "Do you know who he is?"

Gamble looks at it for at least ten seconds and then says, "No, I don't think so. Should I?"

I shrug. "I have no idea."

I leave without telling Joey Gamble what I might or might not do.

I do that for two reasons, the main one being that I don't know what I might or might not do. Laurie is going to want me to take the case, but I just might take a stand and refuse her outright. I also just might be named Miss Congeniality in the next Miss New Jersey contest.

The other reason I don't feel obligated to tell Gamble my intentions is that I don't think he cares one way or the other. He sees me as just another public defender, and I doubt that he feels he has enough information to choose between us.

He actually thinks another lawyer might be as good as me. That in itself might make him a candidate for an insanity defense.

I believed what Gamble told me, though it might be more accurate to say that I didn't disbelieve him. They are both singularly meaningless statements, since I have learned over the years that my instincts in judging guilt or innocence are to be trusted or disregarded, and I never know which until the facts are in.

I have no desire to embark on a murder trial; it takes total focus and an enormous amount of time and effort. But I've been saying that for a long time, and for some reason I keep taking them. Maybe I should spend more time talking to a shrink than to a judge.

But as much as I would dread the process, my real fear is that I'll take the case, get heavily into it, and then learn an explanation for George Adams having Truman that has nothing to do with the Haley murder. That would be an unmitigated disaster, because Adams and Truman represent the only reasons I am considering getting involved at all, and the only reasons I am doubting Joey Gamble's guilt.

I simply do not want to discover that I am representing a murderer, and there is every likelihood that I would find out that I am after it's too late to extricate myself ethically.

Laurie's wanting me to do it will be an important factor, but not because I would be loath to say no to her. The truth is that her reason will be the same as mine: the circumstances are such that we want to know what really happened, and we want to see justice done.

The other truth is that she and I and our team are the only available players that combine the expertise, dedication, and especially resources to make sure the truth will come out.

Or maybe, despite our expertise, dedication, and resources, the truth won't come out. We won't know until we know, and maybe not even then.

When I get home, Laurie is of course anxious to hear how my conversation with Gamble went, and I promise her I will fill her in as soon as I get back from a walk with Tara and Sebastian. She knows I do my best, and often only, thinking while I walk them, so she doesn't offer to come along.

We have two basic walking routes from our house on Forty-second Street in Paterson. One is to walk neighborhood streets on Nineteenth Avenue down to Vreeland Avenue and then come back up on Eighteenth. The other is to head for Eastside Park and then take a slower and more leisurely walk through the park.

I'm sure Tara and Sebastian prefer the

park route, since there are clearly many more smells to savor. And that's the one we take now, since I want to be able to take the time to think things through.

As we are finally leaving the park and heading home, I say to Tara, "So what should I do?"

She turns toward me with a look that says either, "I have no idea what you should do," or "Andy, go with your gut; I'm sure you'll make the right decision," or "I am a dog and don't understand a single word that you just said."

"Thanks, Tara," I say. "That clears it right up."

When we get back to the house, Laurie asks, "What are you going to do?" She knows that the purpose of this particular walk was to make my decision, and for all our joking about it, she respects that it is my decision to make.

"The son of a bitch paid to have Truman killed," I say.

"Yes, he did."

"We've got ourselves a client."

"Good."

"We'll need to get the team together."

She nods. "I've already called everybody."

"Are you controlling me again?"

"I think of it as anticipating your every need."

"I like the sound of that."

Billy Cameron is incredibly excited that I'm taking over the Joey Gamble case.

I can tell because he keeps saying, "This is great . . . this is great," and because he doesn't even mention his touchdown catch against Auburn once.

"You do know that whatever your fee is, Joey can't pay it, right?"

"I understand," I say. "Can you send me whatever additional discovery you've gotten and direct the prosecutor to start sending it to me?"

"Sure," he says. "No problem." Then, "Well, maybe I shouldn't say 'no problem.' "

That sets off an alarm bell. "Why not?"

He hesitates. "They executed a search warrant on Joey's house. I don't think that was in the original material I sent you."

The bells are ringing louder, with some alarm sirens thrown in. "No, it wasn't. What did the search turn up?"

"Some of Haley's property was buried behind Joey's garage, and there was a thirty-eight with it. They're doing a forensics analysis on it now."

"Let me guess. The murder weapon was a thirty-eight."

"Yeah."

"Did I just take on a guilty client?"

"Everybody is entitled to a good defense, Andy."

When I don't answer, he says, "Speaking of good defense, did I mention that the Auburn defensive back I beat wound up playing six games for the Oakland Raiders?"

I get off the phone with a pit in my stomach the size of a tractor trailer. Yes, everyone is entitled to a good defense, but that doesn't mean I have to do the defending. And yes, I know at least as well as anyone that there are two sides to every story, but I also know that one side is almost always bullshit.

I don't like to be on the bullshit side.

I should have told Billy that I changed my mind, but something prevented me from doing it. The deciding factor in taking on the case remains the deciding factor even after the phone call. Truman was owned by James Haley, a murder victim. He wound up in the possession of George Adams, a murderer.

Those are facts, but there are also facts in the discovery documents that implicate Joey Gamble. Those two sets of facts need to be reconciled, and they apparently need to be reconciled by me.

I make another trip down to the jail to talk to Gamble. He sees me and says, "I guess you decided."

I nod. "I did. I'm your lawyer, if you want me. It's your call."

"I'm good with it," he says. "I checked you out."

"How did you do that?"

"I asked my grandmother, and she looked you up on the computer. She said you're a big shot, and that you never lose."

"Everybody loses," I say. "They found some of James Haley's stuff buried behind your garage."

"No way, man."

"And there was a gun with it."

"Hey, come on. Is this some kind of test? I thought you were on my side."

"It's not a test; it's in the police report."

"Then they're lying. I didn't take nothing from that guy, and I don't own a gun."

"Here's what I want you to do. I want you to write down everything that happened the day of the murder. What you did and what you saw. Don't leave out a thing and don't rush; think about it and give me as much detail as you can."

"Somebody is setting me up," he says.

"Who would want to do that?"

"I don't know."

"When you're done writing down what happened that day, think about who it might be."

"Am I going down for this?" he asks, the fear evident in his voice.

"You're sitting here in handcuffs, Joey. You're already down. We're about to start digging you out."

There's a house on East Thirty-ninth Street in Paterson that is going to be empty for a while.

For one thing, while it is in a reasonably nice residential neighborhood, it's not exactly a hot new area. There are no hip hotels with rooftop bars that twentysomethings are trying to convince bouncers to let them into. There are no restaurants at which you simply can't get a reservation to pay twenty-eight dollars for lobster bisque, nor are there tech companies paying high salaries to talented employees eager to get in the door.

It is Paterson, after all.

The house itself is decent enough, comfortable but basically indistinguishable from those around it. But of course there is one thing it has that its neighbors do not.

It's a murder scene.

I doubt strongly that James Haley's brutal

murder will be listed in the "For Rent" real estate ad for this house. For some reason, events like that are right up there with leaky roofs, flooded basements, and rodent infestations as discouragements to potential renters or buyers.

In any event, Laurie and I are not here to make an offer on the place; we are checking out the murder scene, as we always do when we start a case. I've had a lot of murder cases and therefore have been to a lot of murder scenes, and I can't say I've come to enjoy them. They make me uncomfortable for the same reason they keep away future tenants.

They give me the creeps.

But this is where Laurie and I are now, and on our arrival, it becomes apparent that it's going to be a while before some devious real estate agent can successfully conceal the history of the place. That's because it is guarded by police tape and two of Paterson's finest. They have been alerted to let us in, which turns out to have been unnecessary since one of the officers knows and obviously likes Laurie.

We walk down the driveway and enter the house through the back, since that is apparently the way the killer came in. The lock has been picked and broken by someone who knew what they were doing.

Fifteen feet inside the door is where James Haley breathed his last. That is fairly easy to determine, since that is where his body was found, lying in a large pool of blood. The bloodstain is still on the floor.

"He must have heard the noise of the guy breaking in and come down to see what was going on," Laurie says. "The guy probably fired from the doorway."

"He was shot in the back and then again in the head," I say, having read it in the discovery documents.

She nods. "Right. Haley saw the killer with the gun and turned to run, but couldn't get away." She walks over to the chalk outline of the body. "You see that hole in the floor? My guess is that the head shot happened from above while Haley was down, to make sure he was dead."

"An execution," I say. "By someone with no conscience. Someone who was calm, and who has probably done this before."

"No way to prove that," she says. "But probably true. Did neighbors hear the shots?"

"Nobody has said that they did."

"Which means he was using a silencer, or that no one wanted to get involved in any possible trouble. More likely the former, because the 9-1-1 call was made by a neighbor after he saw Haley's body through the back doorway. That same neighbor claimed not to have heard the shot."

We walk into the main area of the house, which looks like a cyclone went through it. Drawers are open and tossed around, clothing and accessories are everywhere. There are also the unmistakable markings where fingerprints — many of which we know turned out to be Joey Gamble's — were taken.

"If the killer was calm and unhurried back there, he sure changed his approach in here," Laurie says. "Unless he wanted to give that appearance."

I nod, understanding what she means. The signs of robbery are over the top, consistent with someone wanting to make it look like the motive was a robbery, and a frenzied one at that. Of course, it could turn out that the appearance is the reality; there is no way to tell at this point.

"What stolen items did they find in Gamble's house?"

"Haley's wallet, with no cash in it, as well as some jewelry, a watch, and a ring."

We go into the bedroom and Laurie points to a large, professional-looking video camera, which was obviously Haley's, sitting on a table. "That thing is probably more valuable than everything else in here combined," she says. "Why wouldn't the killer take it?"

"Maybe it was too large, and he was afraid he'd be seen with it."

We walk over to the camera and see that there is a small open panel on it. "That must be where the film or tape or whatever they use in cameras now goes," I say. "It's empty."

She nods. "Maybe the police took it for analysis, to see if what was on it implicates anyone."

"It's not likely to help us if it does," I say. "At this point, I can't think of any reason for George Adams to be on any film that Haley took. He's here from Philadelphia; he wouldn't likely be hanging out in downtown Paterson."

"But Joey told you that Haley was filming his interview. That will serve to support his case. He didn't shoot Haley at the back door and then sit down for an interview."

On the way home, Laurie says, "I'm afraid there isn't much about this that looks good."

I do a double take. "You wanted me to take the case."

She nods. "I am keenly aware of that."

I'm not surprised that Laurie has done this about-face. She's an ex-cop, so her natural instincts are to believe that if the police make an arrest, they probably are doing so for a very good reason. Also, when she was in favor of my getting involved, we didn't yet know about the police finding incriminating evidence in Gamble's possession.

"What do you think I should do?" I ask.

"Well, for one thing, you should stop listening to me."

Any urgency for the Philadelphia cops to interview Debra about George Adams has disappeared.

The search for him just took a fairly dramatic swing when his body turned up on the bank of the Passaic River.

Based on media reports, they've probably ruled out that he drowned while out for a swim. For one thing, nobody swims in the Passaic River, and in this case George would have been no exception, seeing as how he had entry and exit bullet wounds in the front and back of his head.

Call it Truman's Revenge.

Of course, while this has effectively eliminated Adams as a target for Andy Carpenter–style legal retribution, it has made me more inclined to entertain the possibility that Joey Gamble is a victim here, and not a perpetrator. Gamble certainly didn't kill Adams; his residence in the jail is a rather ironclad alibi. So at the very least we know that there is a murderer out there, since Adams turned up in the river. It is not that far a logical leap, at least for me, to believe that whoever that murderer is, he, or more likely Adams, killed James Haley.

I know Laurie has called the members of our legal team to inform them that we have a new client. I can picture their reactions to it.

In some cases, like my assistant, Edna, it would have been horror. She prefers not doing any work whatsoever; she makes me look like a dynamo.

Hike Lynch, the other lawyer in the firm, would have been fine with our taking on a client, since he likes earning money. But as the leading pessimist on the planet, he would be sure that our efforts will be for naught and our client will spend the rest of his life in prison.

I call Hike, much as I dread doing so. "Laurie told you about our client?" I ask.

"Yeah. Sounds like a real beauty."

Hike's voice sounds raspy, as if he has a cold. I also think he's exaggerating it, wanting me to ask if he's okay. Therefore, I don't. "He's innocent," I say. "That's the official position of our firm."

"Okay. By the way, sorry about my voice."

"Why are you sorry about your voice?" I ask.

"Bronchitis," he says.

Hike never has a cold; he always self-diagnoses it as bronchitis. "Could have fooled me," I say. "You sound great. When you answered I thought I had reached Frank Sinatra, but then I realized, hey, wait a minute, Sinatra is dead, so it can't be him."

"What do you want, Andy?" Hike asks, meaning he has surrendered the point.

"Can you call and find out who the prosecutor assigned to our case is?"

"I don't have to," Hike says. "He's already called us. It's Dylan Campbell."

"Shit," I say. Campbell is a tough, smart lawyer, but that's not why I'm sorry he's on the case. I've beaten him in a couple of big cases, and he clearly resents it and can't stand me. This, despite the fact that I am lovable.

I don't mind that he hates me; it actually makes it easier for me to goad him during the trial. But he will fight me on things that shouldn't call for a fight, especially in the pretrial stages, thereby making everything a hassle. I find that every year I get older, I am less in the mood for hassles.

"Why did he call?" I ask.

"He wants to meet."

"Okay, good. Please call him and tell him I'm on my way."

There's no doubt what Dylan wants to meet about; he believes that the evidence is such that we are going to plead the case out. He'll take that as a victory, which is why he wants to do it in person rather than over the phone. That way he can savor it.

I'm willing to take the meeting for two reasons. First of all, I am going to deprive him of his triumph, at least for the moment, and I'd like to enjoy it in person. Joey Gamble might well plead guilty later on, but we have not even discussed it yet.

The other reason is that I am going to make a rather unusual discovery request. Dylan will probably refuse, because that's his style, and we'll have to petition the court for relief. If that's the case, we might as well get the process under way.

Dylan greets me in his fake-friendly mode, a sure sign that he thinks he has the upper hand. "Damn, it's good to see you, Andy," he lies. "How long has it been?"

"A couple of years," I say. "Last time I saw you was right after the 'not guilty' verdict in the Tommy Infante case." I take every chance I can to jab Dylan; I want him to be angry at me. It makes him more prone to mistakes.

Dylan literally winces at the memory, but recovers quickly. "Yeah, well, that was then, this is now."

"Beautifully put."

"Are you up to speed yet on the Joey Gamble matter?"

"Getting there."

"I can give you forty years for Gamble, out in thirty. And that's way too generous."

"Stop, I'm starting to get teary-eyed," I say, dabbing my eyes for effect. "When did you become an old softie?"

"The offer is good for exactly one week, then we go to trial."

I pretend to fiddle with my watch. "Exactly one week," I say. "Let me set my alarm."

"I think we're done here," he says.

"Not quite. A guy named George Adams was found murdered today in the Passaic River. That case has a bearing on ours, so I want discovery related to him as well."

He smiles. "Right . . . the dog thing. What is it with you and dogs?"

"They provide unconditional love, though in your case they might put some conditions on it." I'm not surprised that he knows about Truman and our view of Adams's connection to him. Pete, being a good and careful cop, would have put it in the file.

Dylan, unfortunately being a good and careful lawyer, would have read it.

"Why would I want to give you that?" Dylan asks.

"Because if you don't, I'll get the court to force you to. And you'll look as if you are not seeking to find the truth."

He thinks about it, no doubt realizing that I will ultimately get what I want. The court would only require us to present some evidence that Adams relates to our case, and Debra's testimony should suffice.

Leeway is given to the defense in matters like this, since it really doesn't hurt the other side, and takes away a possible avenue of appeal later on. Whether we can ultimately get information about Adams admitted at trial remains to be seen, but depriving us of discovery is not something the court would reasonably consider.

I can almost see all this going through Dylan's mind, and it results in a shrug. "Sure, why not? Knock yourself out."

It's a meeting I preferred not to have, at least not in this decade.

The team is back together, and not for a karaoke night or a birthday party. It's because we have a case, which means we are about to start a long, arduous, and uncertain process.

Although as awful as the prospect is, I'd still rather do this than karaoke. I'd rather have a root canal and go on an all-asparagus diet than do karaoke. I'd rather become a Dallas Cowboys cheerleader than do karaoke. Scuba diving versus karaoke would be a tough call.

The meeting is in my office space, which consists of three rooms . . . my private office, Hike's office, and a reception area/ conference room. The setup is not typical of a big-time law firm, since very few big-time law firms sit atop a fruit stand on Van Houten Street in Paterson.

At one point, back when I thought of myself as a practicing attorney, I considered moving to a larger space. We couldn't have done so in this building, because the rest of it is the fruit stand on the first floor, run by our landlord, Sofia Hernandez.

She might have been willing to sell if I offered enough money, but what we would be gaining in space and comfort would be offset by our not having access to perfectly ripe cantaloupes.

Hike Lynch and Sam Willis are both here. Hike will assist me during the trial and write most of the briefs and positions we have to submit to the court. He's outstanding at it. Sam's computer skills make him our entire "cyber-investigative" unit.

Edna is also here, and she approaches me before we begin. "Andy, I need to talk to you about something."

"Sure, Edna," I say, trying not to cringe. I hate talks that "need" to happen.

"I'm here and I'll see this through, but if we're going to keep taking on clients like this, I'm going to have to consider retirement."

I'm not sure how to react to this. Edna hasn't done any actual work in years, unless one considers cashing checks to be work. It's a credit to her work ethic that she never asked me to set up direct deposit.

I nod. "I understand what you're saying. If you have to work, you're going to stop working, and if you don't have to work, you'll continue working."

She thinks about this for a few moments, then says, "I guess that's right; I hadn't thought about it that way."

"Edna, you're an inspiration to us all."

Laurie is of course also present, since she is our main investigator. Willie Miller is here as well, though he has no specific role to play, other than to be supportive and available. Willie has a couple of qualities that I lack: he is both fearless and tough as nails.

The only team regular not present is Marcus Clark, aka Superman. Marcus is a private investigator who serves two functions. He helps Laurie on the detecting stuff, and keeps me alive when I get myself into dangerous situations. Marcus is the single scariest and toughest person on the planet, which is why I have structured it so that he reports to Laurie and not to me. Willie is a black belt in karate and willing to demonstrate it in a fight, but Marcus makes him look like a delicate flower.

Laurie assures me that Marcus will be working on our case, but today he had another commitment. She doesn't say what it is; it could be anything from lifting a bus to invading Venezuela.

"Our client's name is Joey Gamble," is how I start the meeting. It's not a necessary identification, since Sam, Hike, and Laurie already know Gamble's name. Willie and Edna couldn't care less what his name is. "He's accused of murdering James Haley. Haley was gunned down in the house he was renting on Thirty-ninth Street."

I go on to tell the group what we know so far, which obviously isn't much. The highlights, or, more accurately, the lowlights, concern Gamble's fingerprints being found at the murder scene, and the murder weapon and other items belonging to Haley being found at Gamble's house.

"Our client has an explanation for the fingerprints, but is in the dark as to how the stolen merchandise and weapon made their way to his house. It will be up to us to uncover the reason."

I also talk about George Adams and his potential involvement. He is really on the periphery at the moment, which is ironic, since he is the main reason we are on the case at all.

"Laurie, we need to check into something. Gamble told me that Haley was asking him questions about his life in the neighborhood generally, but specifically about someone named Chico Simmons. I assume Simmons is a local gang guy, because Gamble seemed afraid of him. Gamble said that when he had nothing to say about Simmons, Haley seemed to lose interest and concluded the interview."

Laurie nods. "Okay. Maybe Marcus is already familiar with him."

The group asks some questions, very few of which I can answer. We are in the very early stages; the purpose of the meeting is really just to get everyone prepared and focused.

Hike asks if I have discussed a possible plea arrangement with Gamble, and I see Edna perk up at the question. Edna is a big fan of pretrial pleadings; a murder trial involves much less work if there is no actual trial.

"I'm going to talk to him right after this meeting," I say.

"So it's possible that he'll plead?" Edna asks.

"Hang on to the hope, Edna. Hang on to the hope."

Fat Tony Longo was pissed, so much so that he demanded a meeting.

Silvio wasn't used to caving to demands, but in this case he made an exception. Fat Tony was going to be a more significant player than most of the people in Silvio's patchwork-but-growing organization, and the Philadelphia territory was an important one.

Besides, Silvio was smart enough to recognize that Fat Tony had a legitimate beef.

They met in Fat Tony's office in the back room of a restaurant he owned and ate in every night. It was three o'clock in the afternoon, so there were no patrons to accidentally get in the way. The attendees were Fat Tony, Silvio, and an enormous goon whose sole function in life was to protect Fat Tony. The goon stood off to the side, just barely in Silvio's peripheral vision.

"You don't kill my people without me

signing off on it," Fat Tony said. "It is not done, and it is sure as hell not done to me. George was one of my top men."

"George was an asshole," Silvio said, not about to back down. "If stupidity was a disease, he would have died of it long ago. And if he was one of your top men, you might want to change the way you do your recruiting."

"What did he do?" Fat Tony asked. "What the hell did he do that you had to kill him?"

"He jeopardized the operation. He set someone else up to take the fall, without permission. So now there will be a trial and a bunch of lawyers will be looking into it, when that did not have to happen. And then he really screwed up by taking a damn dog."

"A dog?" Fat Tony asked. "What are you talking about?"

"Doesn't matter anymore."

"And his wife? You had to kill her? I knew her; what did she do?"

"She married stupid, which means she was stupid. I don't leave loose ends."

"Next time, and there better not be a next time, you come to me," Fat Tony said.

"You're starting to get on my nerves," Silvio said. "You should be apologizing to me for sticking me with Adams. But I'm telling you now, do . . . not . . . push . . . me."

Out of the corner of his eye, Silvio saw the goon start toward him, apparently conditioned to take exception to insults and threats to his boss.

So fast that neither the goon nor Fat Tony realized what was happening, a gun appeared in Silvio's hand, and in one smooth motion he whirled and shot the goon in the arm, sending him reeling backward. He sank to a sitting position against the wall, holding on to his bloody arm.

"What the . . ." Big Tony managed.

"It's in his arm; I shot his left one because he's right handed," Silvio said. "I could have just as easily put the bullet in his heart; the huge piece of shit should be thanking me for letting him live."

Silvio stood up and pointed the gun at the goon, who was still sitting against the wall. This time he was pointing it at his head, and moving forward. It would be really tough to miss. "Thank me. Thank me," he demanded.

"Hey, come on," Fat Tony said. It took a lot to shock him, but he was shocked at Silvio's behavior. The goon, for his part, said nothing.

"THANK ME!" Silvio screamed, gripping the gun tighter. He was projecting a crazed image for effect, but was actually under complete control.

"Thank him," counseled Fat Tony.

"Thank you," the goon said softly.

Silvio had come into the meeting with some understanding of Fat Tony's position, but that had by now officially been replaced by a cold anger.

He put the gun away and turned back to Fat Tony, speaking more softly and under control. "Maybe you don't understand the situation," he said. "I am in charge of this operation. If you want out, I can find ten people to take your place tomorrow. And then you can go back to taking fifty-dollar bets on Eagles games. Just say the word — no hard feelings."

"I'm staying in," Fat Tony said. "I just want to be treated with respect."

"Then I'll tell you what. You stop sending me stupid people, and I'll stop killing them."

Gamble is upset. "Forty years? For something I didn't do? Why are you asking me to do that?"

"I'm not asking you to do that; if I were you, I wouldn't. But I have to tell you the offer; it's part of my job."

"I won't do it," he says. "I'm twenty damn years old. By the time I got out, I'd be your age."

"Thanks a lot," I say. Joey is adding a couple of decades to my age; he's either not thinking clearly from the stress, or I need to take Laurie's advice and start working out and maybe even eating vegetables. On the other hand, there's nothing wrong with looking old and distinguished.

But for now I say, "So we need to get to work."

" 'We'? What can I do?"

"You didn't take Haley's wallet and jewelry, did you?"

"I told you I didn't."

"And you didn't bury the murder weapon behind your house, did you?"

"No," he says, obviously annoyed. "None of that stuff was at my house. They lied."

I shake my head. "Yes, it was there, and no, they didn't lie. But if you didn't put it there, somebody else did. We need to figure out who, and I need your help on that."

"I don't know who put it there."

"Maybe you do, and you don't realize it. For instance, why would they choose you to set up for killing Haley? What makes you special?"

He think for a short while and then says, "Because I went to his house. They knew my fingerprints would have to be there."

I nod. "Exactly. So who knew you were going there? Who did you tell? And who might those people have told?"

"I've got to think about it."

"Good. You've got plenty of time. Like I told you before, write down everything that comes to your mind so you won't forget it. And while you're at it, write about all the people you hang out with, and have connections to. Especially that guy you mentioned . . . Chico Simmons."

I can see him react with concern at the mere mention of Simmons's name. But he finally nods his agreement, so I continue. "And if you've ever done anything bad in your life, I want to know about it. I won't — I can't — reveal anything you tell me. But you can be sure that things will come out, and we can't afford to have me surprised by them."

"I've never done anything bad."

"Now you can add lying to me to the list. I mean it — no bullshitting."

"Okay," he says.

This has not been a fun conversation for him. It's not a barrel of laughs for me either. I could easily be talking to — or, even worse, representing — a murderer. The only reason I have to doubt his guilt is the fact that George Adams, who we have been unable to connect to Gamble or the murder victim, happened to bring his dog to my vet.

What if Debra was wrong and the guy who brought Truman in wasn't even George Adams? She saw him for maybe five minutes.

As I'm about to leave, Gamble asks me if I'll talk to his grandmother.

"What about?"

"She's worried and she wants to make sure I'm going to be okay."

"I can't promise her that," I say. This is getting worse and worse; I had to get a client with a grandmother?

"I know. But maybe you can tell her that we have a chance?"

"Okay."

"A good chance?" he asks.

"Don't push it. Have her call me."

I leave the jail and am on the way to my car when I hear a woman's voice call out, "Mr. Carpenter!" I look over and see a woman approaching me. She's probably in her sixties, short and a bit overweight. I couldn't be any surer that she's Joey Gamble's grandmother if she were wearing a sandwich board that read, "I'm Joey Gamble's grandmother."

"You're Joey's grandmother," I say.

She nods. "Cynthia Gamble. And you're his lawyer. What are you going to do for my boy?"

"My best."

"Will that be good enough?"

"I don't know yet."

"Mr. Carpenter, I lost my daughter, Joey's mother, in childbirth. I don't know where his father is, but I hope the asshole has been dead a long time. He left when he found out my girl was pregnant. So I have known Joey, taken care of Joey, for every second of his life."

I interrupt. "Mrs. Gamble —"

She returns the interruption, which is just as well, since I had no idea how to finish that sentence. "So I am telling you I know him. I know him as well as I know myself. He could never kill anyone. He could never hurt anyone."

"I understand."

"So now that I am telling you, you need to tell everyone else. I am depending on you, and I don't like to have to depend on anyone. But you need to make them understand." She pauses, and I think she's about to cry, but she takes the time to compose herself. This is one tough lady. "Please. Please make them understand."

"Marcus is a father," Laurie says, as I walk in.

If you had asked me, I would have thought it just as likely that her first sentence would have been, "We're having dinner on Pluto tonight."

"There's a baby Marcus in the world?" I ask. I had no idea his wife was pregnant, but I assume Grandpa Jor-El must be very proud.

"Not exactly. Jeannie had a little girl; they named her Brandy. Mother and daughter are doing fine. That's why he wasn't at the meeting; he didn't want me to tell anyone until after the birth."

I've only met Jeannie Clark once, at a victory party after one of our trials. She's short and perky and bubbly, which makes her the exact opposite of her husband. But she must be a force to be reckoned with; no one else in the world could refer to Marcus as "my little Markie."

An image of Marcus at a Lamaze class just popped into my head. He's yelling, "Breathe!" and every woman in the class is so scared that they're breathing like crazy. I know I'd breathe if Marcus told me to; hell, if he yelled loud enough, I'd give birth.

"I wouldn't want to be the first guy that tries to date that kid," I say. "If Marcus told me to get her home by ten o'clock, we'd sit on the front porch for the whole time to make sure we weren't late."

"He sounded really happy; he said she was adorable."

I have no idea how Laurie understands a single word Marcus says; I certainly don't. To me they sound like unintelligible, and very rare, one-syllable grunts. But Laurie sees him as another Winston Churchill.

I do have one worry. "Is this going to make him more cautious . . . you know, in his work?" My unvoiced concern, of course, is that he would be less willing to take risks in the protection of yours truly. I could replace him, of course, but it would mean hiring an entire marine battalion.

"Marcus?" she asks. "I don't think so. You're safe."

"Good. When is he coming back to work?"

"Right away. I asked him to find out

whatever he can about Chico Simmons, and he said he already knows a lot about him. He'll talk to us tomorrow."

"Okay. Good."

Laurie comes with me on my evening walk with Tara and Sebastian, and I use the time to update her on my talk with our client, as well as my encounter with his grandmother. "I don't do well with grandmothers," I say. "I'm better with juries."

"I can't imagine what this must be like for her. To raise him like that, to love him, and then to see him in this situation. She must feel so helpless."

"She doesn't come across as the helpless type," I say. "But she is scared. I don't think she has a hell of a lot of trust in the system, or in me, for that matter."

"Wait until she hears that her grandson's fingerprints were at the murder scene, and the victim's possessions and the murder weapon were at his house."

"She'll have to read it in the paper," I say. "I'm sure not telling her."

"I was looking at the forensic reports," Laurie says. "George Adams's prints were not in Haley's house. If he was there, he must have been wearing gloves."

"Damn," I say. "Why didn't I think of that?"

"What?"

"Adams's prints. You're right — they weren't at the murder scene because he was wearing gloves. But he wouldn't have been wearing gloves at the vet's office when he signed the euthanasia form."

"Where is it?"

"Dowling still has it; Debra gave it to him, and he said he was keeping it in the office safe. It's worth a shot. If we can get those prints, then we will know for sure it was him with Truman."

I'd like to hurry back home to put this into motion, but Sebastian has other ideas. He is very particular about where he will piss, and also moves incredibly slowly. He doesn't exactly plod; it's slower than that. He sort of oozes, like slow-moving, hairy lava.

But we finally make it back, and I call Dowling, who confirms that the euthanasia form is still in his safe. I tell him not to touch it, and that we will have someone there in the morning to try to get finger-prints off of it.

Meanwhile, Laurie is on the phone with Rob Flory, a retired cop who worked with her on the police force. Rob was in forensics and is occasionally called upon by lawyers like me as an expert witness. Rob agrees to go to Dowling's office in the morning to do what we need done.

Laurie will go down there as well to make sure that all goes smoothly. She'll also chronicle the whole operation on video so there will be a record of it, though that isn't totally necessary. Flory has a great deal of credibility and would be difficult for Dylan to challenge if he testifies.

I'll be at the arraignment in the morning, but we won't have any answers about the prints in the moment anyway. There will certainly be some prints; it will just be a question of determining whose they are. Flory will be helpful in that also; he'll have friends currently in forensics, most of whom learned under him, who will run the found prints through the system.

Also, the prints will remain on the piece of paper, if they're there in the first place, so the prosecution could always have their own experts examine it.

I'm very hopeful about the possibility of finding Adams's prints, and I say so to Laurie.

She pours a little cold water on it by saying, "Of course, even if Adams's prints are on the form, all it proves is that he had Truman. It doesn't mean he killed Haley, or that Joey didn't."

"True, but it connects Adams to our case, which will make testimony and evidence about him admissible in Joey's trial. Debra's identification of him could be challenged; his prints can't."

"You called your client Joey," she says.

"So?"

"It means you like him. When you don't like someone, you refer to them by their last name."

"Don't analyze me, Collins."

I meet with Joey in an anteroom a half hour before the arraignment.

The purpose is to brief him on what will happen and prepare him for his role in it. The thirty minutes is probably twenty-five more than I need, since almost nothing will happen, and his entire role will likely consist of uttering four words.

Before we go into the courtroom, he tells me that, to the best of his recollection, the only person he told that he was going to see Haley was his best friend, Archie Sandler. He didn't tell Archie that the information was to be kept confidential, though in retrospect he regrets telling anyone.

Haley had not made many friends snooping around with his camera, and Gamble should have realized that some people would not look favorably on his talking to Haley. Of course, he never imagined that any negative feedback could have this kind of result.

Before we head into the courtroom, I ask him how he's doing in the jail and if he needs anything.

"Maybe something to read?"

"You mean like magazines?" I ask.

"That's fine, but I'd really like some books."

"What kind?"

"Historical nonfiction is my favorite." I must have some kind of reaction, because he smiles and adds, "I'm a nerd."

Judge Madeline Matthews is handling the arraignment, which means she will likely be presiding at trial. In relative terms, this is a positive. Passaic County judges can be ranked into three basic groups. There are those who despise me, those who dislike me a great deal, and those who aren't crazy about me but don't recoil when I'm in their courtroom.

Judge Matthews falls into this last category. She's smart and fair, and while she won't put up with too much of my bullshit, she'll tolerate it longer than most. Put another way, she probably views me with contempt, but probably won't charge me with it.

Hike is waiting for us at the defense table when we arrive. I introduce him to Joey, and Hike and I flank him on his left and right. Hike leans across Joey to say to me, "It's Judge Matthews." Then he shakes his head. "Not good . . . not good."

Fortunately I've already warned Joey about Hike's unerring ability to see and even predict the worst possible outcome in all situations, so hopefully he is discounting Hike's view of Judge Matthews.

Sitting behind our table is Cynthia Gamble, Joey's grandmother. I nod to her, but she just stares me down. This is a woman who demands a total victory and will tolerate nothing less. I have got to come up with a way to make sure she doesn't talk to Hike.

The judge calls on Dylan to recite the charges that the State of New Jersey is throwing at Joey. He is facing murder in the first degree, which carries a maximum sentence of life imprisonment. I can feel Joey react as Dylan talks; he must realize that he is staring down the possibility of his life being essentially over.

It appears that Judge Matthews will, in fact, also be handling the trial, since she schedules the date by consulting her own calendar. Eventually she calls on Joey to offer his plea, and he does so in a voice trying to be forceful, but quavering a bit.

"Not guilty, Your Honor."

I ask that bail be set and of course Dylan is firmly opposed. I have no chance to win this argument, and Judge Matthews quickly rejects our position. Defendants on trial for murder one do not get out on bail.

Once court is adjourned and Joey is taken away, Dylan comes over to me. "Things have changed; the offer is only good until close of business today."

"Close of which business?" I ask. "Some businesses are open later than others. There's a McDonald's on Route 4 that's open all night."

"Five P.M."

"Got it. We should synchronize our watches."

He doesn't consider that worthy of a reply and heads back to his prosecution team. Dylan is practically salivating at the prospect of taking this to trial, and at this point I can't say that I blame him.

When I get back to the house, Marcus is sitting in the kitchen with Laurie, having coffee. "Marcus, congratulations," I say. "Wonderful news."

"Yunh," he says. Marcus is obviously so excited that he's verbally gushing.

"Any pictures of the baby?"

"Yunh," he says, but makes no effort to show me any. Instead, Laurie takes his phone and shows me a few. The baby is in fact adorable and doesn't look tough or scary. I wonder briefly what Marcus's own baby pictures looked like, and then I realize that I don't want to know.

"Marcus has just given me his report on Chico Simmons," she says. "He's heading back to the hospital, so I'll tell you about it."

I'm relieved to hear this, because any verbal report from Marcus requires subtitles for me to understand it. Once he leaves, Laurie fills me in.

"Chico Simmons, at least until now, has been a typical street gang leader. He has his people and his turf, nothing unusual. Except he's a bit more ruthless than most."

"How so?"

"Well, his gang is called X. That's it — just 'X.' But the way he came up with the name is the story. Maybe it's a myth to frighten his enemies, or maybe not. There's no way to be sure."

"What's the story?" I ask.

"A few years ago, someone was trying to intrude on his turf. So his people grabbed the guy one night and took him to where Chico does business from. It's apparently a warehouse on Bergen Street. They tied the guy to a chair, and Chico came in. Chico had a marker with him, and he drew an X in the middle of the guy's forehead.

"Then, while the guy begged for his life, Chico calmly took out his gun and from about two feet away put a bullet right where the X was."

"Sounds like a fun guy," I say. "But you said he was a typical street gang leader 'until now.' What did you mean?"

"A couple of things. As more traditional organized crime figures have gone down, either as a result of violence or convictions, vacuums have been created that guys like Simmons are anxious to fill. Then, according to Marcus, Simmons has somehow gotten his hands on enough money to entice his street opponents to join him. He's been able to consolidate his power and expand."

"Where did he get the money?"

She shrugs. "Marcus doesn't know, but you can be sure it's not from wise investments, or an expanding 401(k)."

"Is Marcus aware of any connection between Simmons and Haley, or Simmons and Adams?"

"Not yet, but most of what I told you was things he already knew. He's just getting into our case now; he doesn't really know anything helpful yet."

"I know the feeling."

Carol Mehlman's sister Denise was married to George Adams.

He's wanted for Denise's murder, or at least he was until his body turned up in the Passaic River. That doesn't mean he didn't kill her, but it certainly means he's no longer the target of a manhunt.

Laurie's contact in Philadelphia PD, Sergeant Rubin, had expressed doubt to us that George had killed his wife, saying that leaving her body there like that was not Adams's style. In my view, George's subsequent murder buttresses Rubin's point of view.

While I admit I know very little about Adams, to say nothing of his marriage, the pieces just do not seem to fit. It seems highly unlikely that he would kill his wife, run off to New York, and then be gunned down himself. Could someone be avenging his wife's death that quickly? Who? I don't think this is the explanation.

And that scenario doesn't even take into account Adams possessing Truman, the dog owned by still another murder victim. It clearly does not add up, or if it does, I haven't been able to figure out the math yet.

Laurie has been checking in with Sergeant Rubin periodically, and he's the one who told us about Carol Mehlman. He said that she might have some insight into her sister's death, though that insight is apparently not great, since according to Rubin, the investigation is going nowhere.

Mehlman lives in Freehold, New Jersey, only about an hour's ride from Paterson. I don't expect to learn much from her relating to our case, but it's not that far, and I don't have anything better to do. Besides, I have a nostalgic fondness for Freehold; my father occasionally took me to the harness track there back in the day.

So here I am.

I had called Carol to set up the meeting and she eagerly jumped at the opportunity. I'm not sure why that is yet, but I'll no doubt find out soon. When I pull up to her house, she comes out on her porch to greet me, and her handshake turns into a gesture that just about yanks me into the house.

We set up in her den, and she has coffee brewed and ready. She starts off by saying she's confused about where I fit into this whole thing.

"I can see where you would be," I say. "There's another murder case, in northern New Jersey, that George Adams appears to have some involvement in. Someone else has been accused of that murder, and I am his attorney."

"I'm glad he's dead," she says.

"George?"

She nods. "George. I told Denise, everybody in the family told Denise, stay away from that guy. He was rotten from the inside; if you spent five minutes with him, you would know that. But Denise couldn't see it."

"Do you think he killed her?"

I expect her to say he is as guilty as hell, but she surprises me. "I don't know. He worshiped her. It was the strangest thing, but she just had this ability to control him. Everybody knew what he was out there in the world, but with her, he was different."

"So if he didn't, who did?"

"I don't know. Maybe one of the animals that he dealt with was getting back at him. If you wanted to hurt George, you could do it by hurting Denise. I hated him, but he loved my sister." Then, "And she loved him; she gave up her family to love him."

"Her family turned against her?"

She nods. "All except me. She was my twin sister. We were like one person."

I hadn't realized they were twins. It seems to make the situation sadder and more poignant, but has absolutely nothing to do with why I'm here. In fact, I have no idea why I'm here, other than to find out if Carol can point her finger at another possible killer, at least of her sister.

I'm just trying to accumulate information, any pieces I can find, and I can worry about putting them together later. Too bad they don't always fit.

"I don't think George killed her," Carol says, as if she's making a final decision on the matter. "Not physically. But the world he inhabited killed her as surely as if he did it himself. It was because of him that she had contact with people like that."

As I'm leaving, I think of one more question. "Did your sister and George have a dog?"

She reacts as if I just asked her a more significant question than I realize. "Why do you ask that?"

"I'll tell you, but I'd rather you answer first, if you don't mind. I have my reasons."

She hesitates, but then says, "The day before she died, Denise told me that George had called to say he was bringing home a dog. She had always wanted one, but he had been opposed to it."

"Did she say what kind?"

"Better than that. He sent her a picture and she sent it to me."

"Can I see it?"

She goes to her phone, finds the email, and shows it to me. "Here it is."

It doesn't surprise me that I'm looking at Truman.

I'm very confident we can prove that George Adams had possession of Truman.

Between the chip identifying Truman as James Haley's dog, Debra's clear identification of Adams, and finally to the photographic evidence that Carol Mehlman provided, we should have no trouble making the connection clear enough to satisfy the jury. To turn it into a complete slam dunk, Rob Flory reports to Laurie that Adams's prints are, in fact, on the euthanasia form.

All of this would be great news if this were a civil case involving dog ownership, but it's unfortunately a murder case that seems to have no other connection to Adams. For example, why the hell would Adams come up to New Jersey to kill Haley, and why would his wife be killed in retribution?

And while I'm throwing out questions I can't answer, how would Adams know Joey

Gamble well enough to frame him? He couldn't have followed Joey home from Haley's that night, even if he had seen Joey leaving, because he first went inside to kill Haley.

I'm home tonight and we've just finished dinner when Marcus calls Laurie to tell her that he has Archie Sandler, the friend Joey Gamble says he told about going to see Haley that night. She tells Marcus to hold on while she gives me this news.

"What does that mean, he 'has him'?" I ask. Knowing Marcus, it could mean anything from "sitting in a car with him," to "jangling him by his collar off the roof of a high rise."

She asks him, and the answer comes back that Archie actually is in Marcus's car. "You want him to bring him here?" Laurie asks.

"No. Let's do this at the office." I try not to do things like this at the house much. I started that because I didn't want Ricky exposed to this stuff, but even though he's at camp, I think it's a good practice to continue.

Laurie tells Marcus that I'll meet him at the office in twenty minutes. She offers to go with me, but we agree that it's probably best that she doesn't. We don't know anything about Sandler's demeanor or attitude, and we don't want to overwhelm him.

She's not worried about me going into a potentially dangerous situation because . . . well . . . Marcus. If we were going on a top-secret reconnaissance mission in Yemen, she would not be worried about me because . . . well . . . Marcus.

Marcus and Archie Sandler are already in my office when I get there. Sandler looks to be in his early twenties, so a bit older than his friend Joey Gamble. He's also a good five inches taller and thirty pounds heavier.

He's also scared.

"Hello, Archie. Thanks for coming."

"I don't want to be here." He points to Marcus. "This . . . guy . . . he told me that if I didn't come with him, he'd snap my neck like a twig."

I smile. "He's quite a kidder, isn't he? You should see his stand-up act. You're free to go anytime, but Marcus and I wanted to give you a chance to help your friend."

"What friend?"

"Joey Gamble. I'm his attorney. I've just got a few questions for you."

He doesn't respond to that, so I continue.

"You know who James Haley is, right?"

He nods. "The film guy; the one who got killed."

"Right. The film guy who got killed. Did

you ever meet him?"

"No. He was around that day; he was around for a couple of days. But I didn't talk to him."

"Who did talk to him?"

"A couple of guys. I don't know."

"Did Joey talk to him?"

He nods reluctantly. "Yeah. Joey."

"Do you know what they talked about?"

"No."

"Did Joey tell you he was going to see him at his house that night?" I ask.

"No."

"Archie, this is not going well. Joey already told me that he told you he was going there. I'm Joey's lawyer; if you want to help him, then you should be helping me." I point to Marcus, who has been sitting silently throughout. "And if you cooperate, it will make Marcus very happy. Don't forget the whole neck-twig thing."

"Okay. I knew he was going there."

I nod. "Good. Now we're moving right along. Who did you share that information with?"

"Some guys; I don't remember exactly."

"Archie . . ." I say, using the most admonishing tone I can muster. I could turn to Marcus to help; he may well be the best admonisher in the galaxy.

"I really don't. It was just a few guys; we were standing in front of the 7-Eleven. Hey, I didn't think there was any harm in it. Joey hadn't told me to keep my mouth shut about it. I didn't know the guy was going to get killed."

"Was one of guys you told Chico Simmons?"

Sandler reacts; the name Chico Simmons clearly carries some significant meaning, as it did when I mentioned him to Joey. "No. I don't talk to Chico."

"So you don't know if Chico was aware that Joey was going to see Haley. Might the guys you told have mentioned it to him?"

"Chico knows everything that happens on the street," he says.

"Do you know if Chico met Haley?"

"I don't know. But whether he did or not, he knew about him."

I nod. "Because Chico knows everything that happens on the street. Does he know you're here?"

"If he does, I'm probably a dead man."

I offer to have Marcus drive Archie wherever he wants to go, but he wants nothing more to do with Marcus or me. In fact, he asks for a head start out of the building so he won't be seen with us. I'm okay with that, or I would be if it didn't mean being left alone with Marcus.

Once Archie leaves, the silence in the room is deafening. "How's the baby?" I ask.

"Yunh."

"Glad to hear it."

The Eliot is a boutique luxury hotel on Commonwealth Avenue in Boston.

It is not the type of hotel Frank Silvio would ordinarily choose to stay in. That had nothing to do with the quality of the place, but rather the size. The Eliot has a small lobby and entering means being seen by three bellman and the front-desk people. Silvio prefers large, crowded hotels where anonymity is more easily achieved.

In Silvio's business, and especially in Silvio's situation, being noticed is not a positive.

But this was where Mateo Rojas had instructed him to stay. Silvio was not used to taking instructions, never mind orders, from anyone, but in Rojas's case, he was willing to make an exception.

It was not because Rojas was a scary guy, though he is certainly that. Silvio considered himself a pretty tough and scary guy as well, and he believed he could handle anyone. No, Silvio followed Rojas's instructions because Rojas had an apparently endless supply of money, and a willingness to share it.

When Silvio checked in, as always under an assumed name using a fake ID, he was given a very large old-fashioned metal key on a circular ring. The smiling desk clerk said that the hotel policy was for guests to leave the key at the front desk when they left the hotel and pick it up again on their return.

Silvio returned the smile, but had absolutely no intention of following that policy. With all the cash that would be in the room safe, should he leave the room even for a minute, no one else was going to have that key.

Twenty minutes after checking in, the front desk called to say there was a Mr. Rojas there to see him. He instructed the clerk to send him right up. Silvio had no doubt that Rojas was also not his real name, but it didn't bother him in the slightest.

When Silvio opened the door, no greetings were exchanged. Silvio noted with satisfaction the small suitcase Rojas brought into the room, and knew it wasn't filled with pajamas and toiletries. It was amazing how much money could be contained in a case that size, provided the bills were of large enough denominations.

It was a bit hard to believe that only one month had gone by since he and Rojas had last met; it seemed much longer, perhaps because it had been such an eventful time.

"A lot has happened since the last time we were together," Silvio said.

The man calling himself Rojas nodded. "Some of it good, some bad." As he talked he went to the minibar and took out a sparkling water. Silvio noticed that he was wearing skintight gloves. Because they were flesh colored, they would not call attention to the fact that he was wearing gloves in summer, but they'd prevent him from inadvertently leaving behind fingerprints.

"What does that mean?" Silvio asked.

"You have made mistakes."

"I did what I had to do."

"Violence should be the last resort," Rojas said. "It does not help our business, and it brings unwanted attention."

"Haley was not my fault," Silvio said.

"Everything is your fault," Rojas said. "Employing Adams was a grave mistake. You hired him, so his mistakes are yours. I hired you, so your mistakes are mine. In this case, you should have done the work yourself."

"I can't be everywhere at once."

"You are being paid to be everywhere at once."

"I corrected the Adams mistake." Silvio was getting annoyed at having to defend himself.

"Yes, you did. Which was your next mistake. Adams's body should never have been found. But all of that has already happened. More important is the fact that you are moving too slowly. Two markets is not enough; we are behind schedule."

"That's why I'm here in Boston, and after that Baltimore," Silvio said. "Then I think we should move on to Ohio. I have good connections there."

Rojas shook his head. "East Coast only, as we've discussed."

"Okay. You're the boss." Silvio believed that Rojas might be utilizing other people to cover other areas of the country, but he wasn't about to confront him with it. For the time being, he'd have to stick to the areas he was given. Later? Who knows?

"Yes," Rojas agreed. "I am." Then, without another word, he left the room, leaving the suitcase behind.

"Andy, I think I'm seeing a coincidence here," Laurie says.

That would be like Laurie saying that on the way to the supermarket, she saw the Loch Ness monster. Coincidences are not recognized as possible in our business; we are as likely to run into a real one as the Knicks are to win the NBA Finals this year. Or next year. Or the decade after that.

And if a coincidence should actually happen, well, that's just a coincidence.

"What do you mean?"

"I mean you're a criminal defense attorney and you're known as a dog lover and rescuer. Adams could have brought Truman into any veterinarian in New Jersey, but he brought him to yours. Doesn't that seem at least a little curious?"

"It does," I say, because it certainly does. "But why would Adams possibly have any interest in bringing us into the case? And there was no reason to even think it would. Adams believed Dowling would put Truman down and that would be the end of it."

She nods. "I can't argue with that, but it's still too convenient. Have you been getting discovery on the Adams killing?"

"Yes, but there's not that much. I think it's fair to say that this is not being treated with great importance. Commissions are not being formed to find out who gunned down poor George Adams. No one is looking for the second shooter on the grassy knoll."

"It's still a murder," she says. As a former cop who still thinks like one, it annoys her to hear that a very serious crime like this is not the focus of an intense investigation, no matter who the victim is.

"Yes, but it's one that is probably slipping through the law enforcement cracks. For one thing, Jersey cops have jurisdiction, but what are they looking at? A Philly mobster, a hit man himself, was killed in what looks like a mob hit. The murderer is probably back in Philly now, sucking on a cheese steak. You think cops here are going to solve this?"

She nods in agreement. "And the Philly cops are happy it happened here."

"Right. All they care about is the Denise

Adams hit, not that they are likely to solve that one either. For all we know, they could still be blaming that on hubby George. That would put the entire situation away in a nice little box."

I head down to the Tara Foundation to check on Truman and all the other dogs down there. I've been spending very little time there, which I always feel guilty about. But Willie and Sondra understand the time constraints involved in preparing for a trial, and they are very good about it. It helps that they love what they do.

Willie is feeling pretty good when I get there. He's pleased that Murphy, a mastiff mix that we rescued a few weeks ago, has just been adopted into what Willie views as a very good dog home. Willie has very strict standards about what constitutes an acceptable adopter; if he was okay with this family, then Murphy has done quite well for himself.

"How's Truman?" I ask.

He smiles. "He's a piece of work."

"How so?"

"Well, for one thing, he bit me his second night here."

I'm surprised and not at all happy to hear this. "Bad?"

"Nah, barely broke the skin. But it took

him a while to get used to me. He was fine with Sondra from the beginning. Now he follows me everywhere."

"You think we can place him?" There is always danger involved in placing a dog who bites, to say nothing of the difficulty in finding people who want those kind of dogs.

He nods. "I think so. It'll just take time finding the right home. He's a great dog once he gets to know you."

"Okay, you're calling the shots here."

"I wonder if he bit Adams that night," Willie says. "That would explain him wanting to get rid of him."

I think Willie just solved Laurie's co-incidence question without realizing it. But the important question is not *if* Truman bit Adams that night.

It's *where* he bit Adams that night.

"Adams brought Truman to the vet the day after the murder," I say.

It brings a nod from Laurie and a one-word question: "So?"

"So where did he stay that night? Or any other nights he was here?"

"I have no idea," she says. "Do you?"

"Not exactly, but close. You thought that the reason Adams brought Truman to my vet might have had something to do with me, but it couldn't have. Adams wouldn't have known about me, and he sure as hell wouldn't have known who my vet was. And if he did, he wouldn't have had any reason to care."

"So why that vet?"

"Because of where the office is. It must have been convenient to where Adams was staying. He probably saw the place; he might have driven by a couple of times. Adams just wanted to get rid of Truman; any vet would have done the trick for him. He wouldn't have known one vet from the other up here, so he picked the easiest one."

"So you think that by checking out the hotels within a reasonable radius, we might be able to find out where he was staying?"

I nod. "It's worth a shot. It's very possible that he left some things there that could give us a lead to what the hell is going on. He may have gotten himself killed before he planned to leave, and we know the police haven't located where he was staying because it's not in the discovery. I doubt they're trying very hard."

"There shouldn't be that many possible places near there," Laurie says.

"I agree." Dowling's office is in Glen Rock, which, when it comes to hotels, will never be confused with Las Vegas. "I'll get Sam to work on a list; let's start with a one-mile radius and work out from there as we need to."

"He should also list places that allow dogs, if he has access to the information."

"I'll tell him, though I imagine Adams's decision to take Truman was spur of the moment."

I call Sam and tell him what we need and what we're doing. "So this is a shoe-leather job?" he asks.

"A shoe-leather job? What does that mean?"

"You know, going door to door, asking questions, investigating," he says. "Using shoe-leather the old-fashioned way."

"Right. But Laurie is doing it. I doubt she'll even wear leather shoes, more likely sneakers. So that would probably make it a canvas job, right?"

"Let me help, Andy. I can do this."

"That's okay, Sam."

"Come on, I can ask the same questions. We'll be able to cover it in half the time, and if I get a hit, I'll call you and Laurie."

It's not a bad idea; I don't really see how Sam could screw it up, though I recognize that Sam could definitely screw it up. He does considerably better in the cyber world than the real world. "Okay," I say.

"Great."

"Sam, no shooting, and no citizen's arrests."

"I won't even bring my gun. Or maybe I will, just in case, but I won't load it. Or maybe I'll load it, but I'll keep the safety on."

"Sam . . ."

"Okay, okay." Sam says he'll get right on the list, and with the prospect of doing a shoe-leather job waiting for him when he finishes, I have no doubt that it will be quick.

That should give me time to write a letter to Ricky at camp, which I am embarrassed to say I haven't done for three days. I have absolutely nothing new to say, so I stick with the old standards of asking him how it's going, telling him how much I miss him, how much fun I hope he's having, blah, blah, blah.

I also include information about the Mets, since we're both fans, but that runs the risk of the letter getting too depressing. This is another in a series of "rebuilding" years for the Mets. The pyramids took less years getting built.

But I do promise to take Ricky to a game when he gets home, so I think the letter will be reasonably well received. I hope so; coming up with these things takes a lot of work.

Sam shows up about two hours after I gave him the assignment. There just aren't that many places that Adams could have stayed, so Sam has extended the radius to five miles rather than one. Even with that, there are only twenty-six possibilities.

Laurie will take half and Sam the other half. We spend an hour carefully instructing Sam on what he should say when he visits each place, and he swears that he will do exactly as instructed. "No improvising," he swears.

This may well come to nothing, but for the moment it is all we have. Should we get lucky, we're going to have to be prepared. To that end, Laurie makes some phone calls to friends with an invitation and request for them to join our team, should they be needed.

They all agree, both out of friendship to Laurie and at the promise that they will be well paid for their efforts.

If we call on them, it will either be money well spent or money poured down the drain.

We'll know when we know.

The ship sailed under a Chechen flag.

The crew carried Chechen passports, none of which were real, and all of which misstated their nationality.

They approached the coast near dusk and paused slightly more than three miles from land, staying just outside the territorial waters of the United States.

Once they reached that position, the men on deck signaled a request to the captain, who scanned the horizon before giving them permission to proceed.

Once that was accomplished, the ship went on to the Bahamas and docked in Nassau, there to unload its supplies of produce and household goods.

They would be back the following week, just as they were every week, occasionally even more often than that. They would be on a different ship, under a different flag, and with different passports.

But with the same mission.
That never changed.

"Andy, I found the place. I know where he stayed."

I can hear the excitement in Sam's voice as he reports this. It's the second day that he and Laurie have been out there, and I was beginning to think they were wasting their time. Of course, what Sam's telling me is a long way from being confirmed.

"Where are you?"

The Park Village garden apartments on Cedar Avenue in Hawthorne. It's just under two miles from the vet's office, but you have to pass by there to get to the highway, or to Paterson. Adams must have passed it a bunch of times if he did any driving.

"Are you there now?" I ask.

"Yes. I'm with the manager of the place, Tommy Halitzky; we're in his office. He's even heard of you; he's seen you on television."

"Stay right there," I say. "Call Laurie and

tell her to meet us there in fifteen minutes, and tell her to put the team on alert."

"What team?"

"She'll know." I don't want to keep this conversation going too long; I want to get there and see what we have. "I'm on my way, Sam."

It takes me twenty minutes to get to the address in Hawthorne, and when I pull up to the manager's office in front, I see that Laurie's car is already there. She's been canvassing hotels in the area as well, so was obviously close by.

I enter the office and Laurie, Sam, and a guy I can safely assume to be Tommy Halitzky look up. Halitzky is at his desk and Laurie and Sam are in the two chairs across from it.

"Here he is," says Sam. "Looks just like he does on television, huh?"

"That's because I use the same face for my TV appearances. Hello, Mr. Halitzky," I say. "Andy Carpenter."

We shake hands and I turn to Laurie. "So bring me up to date."

"Mr. Halitzky has made a positive investigation of Mr. Adams based on the photograph we showed him."

Halitzky nods. "I'm sure of it."

Laurie continues, "He reports that Mr.

Adams, using the name Charles Henderson, rented the apartment for one week and paid in cash. He stayed here for three or four days, Mr. Halitzky cannot be sure exactly how long, and then wasn't seen again. He left behind some possessions, which remain in the apartment. There are other vacancies, so it was not necessary to remove them."

Halitzky nods. "I thought he might come back. The guy owes me money now."

I nod. "Understood. We'll pay any back rent that he owes."

Halitzky brightens at this. "Great."

"All we ask is that we have access to the apartment so we can examine the materials. We'll be bringing in qualified experts to supervise the process. And nothing will be lost or destroyed; as an officer of the court, I can personally guarantee that."

Halitzky nods vigorously. "Sure. No problem. That's good enough for me." I can pretty much say anything and he'll buy it. This is one smart guy.

"Great. We appreciate your cooperation." I turn to Laurie. "Let's get started."

She nods. "I've already made the calls. They'll be here in a few minutes."

So we wait. It gives me time to regale Halitzky with inside stories about some of the news personalities who have interviewed me on television. I have absolutely nothing interesting to say about any of them, since all I do is sit there and answer their questions. But Halitzky seems fine just basking in my reflected glory.

I like this guy a lot.

It takes about forty-five minutes for Mark Jamieson to arrive. I introduce him to Halitzky and Sam as Lieutenant Mark Jamieson, since that was his rank when he left the Paterson PD. He and Laurie go back a long way, though he stayed on the force for a number of years longer than she did.

Jamieson, like Laurie, has kept active by doing private investigative work, which is what he is technically doing for us now.

Five minutes later, Sergeant Rob Flory shows up. He's the ex-forensics cop who got the fingerprints off the euthanasia form. We're going to need his services again right now.

We have no idea what we will find in Adams's room, or whether any of it will be of value to us. But if we get lucky, then all evidence must be able to survive prosecution challenges as to legitimacy, chain of custody, etc.

Flory and Jamieson can accomplish this for us. Between their involvement, and the fact that we are going to be careful and do everything by the book, we can accomplish our task of both preserving the evidence and keeping it secret until we are ready to reveal it.

That's assuming, of course, that any evidence is here.

The team is ready, and everyone has a role, even Sam.

Flory is going in first, and he will dust for fingerprints and look for any other forensic evidence that can be found. He's just one person with limited equipment, but he'll do the best he can.

The purpose of the fingerprinting is to provide proof that Adams really stayed here. If we find any other prints that can help us, that will be a bonus, but we're not expecting to.

Once that is accomplished, Laurie and I will go through everything, under the watchful eye of Jamieson. If we come up with anything interesting, then we'll photograph it. All originals will stay with Jamieson, who will place the materials in evidence bags and store them in a safe, secure area.

Sam's role is to document everything, all the evidence collection and the entire search, on video. He begins the process by recording Halitzky saying on camera that we have his full permission to enter, since the tenant is behind on his rent. The terms of the rental agreement permit the entering and even the seizure of possessions.

I don't believe that anything we find needs to be shared with the prosecution, at least for now. They have refused to acknowledge that Adams is even tangentially involved with the Haley murder, mocking the connection through Truman.

But if we get lucky and come up with something, we will want to share it and then introduce it at trial. If that happens, we will have had to do everything by the book, which is why Jamieson and Flory are here. Their credibility, plus the care with which all of this is handled, will make it difficult to challenge.

We all go into Adams's apartment and introduce ourselves to Sam's video. I explain in detail exactly what is about to happen, and how the evidence will be handled.

And now we begin.

The first thing we notice is that Adams clearly intended to come back here. All his clothes are here, as is his suitcase. There is also some food in the refrigerator and in the small cupboard. Most of it is snack-type food . . . chips, pretzels, chocolate-covered raisins, soda . . . Adams was not a healthy eater. There are no peas to be found.

Unfortunately, there isn't much of anything to be found. There's not a signed confession or any apparent hint why he was there. Nor is there any obvious connection to Haley, or any weapons.

There is a briefcase, but all that is in it is a blank pad of paper and two pens. It has a lock on it, but is open.

Flory reports that he has found at least a dozen different fingerprints, all of which he is carefully documenting. That in itself is not significant; this apartment is a short-term rental and most of those fingerprints could be previous tenants. Flory will run them all through the database; he has friends in the department who will give him access without broadcasting it to their bosses.

I point to the hardwood floor. "That looks like dog hair. Let's get some, and we can compare it to Truman's."

"You're going to compare dog hair?" Flory asks, clearly doubting the significance.

"Absolutely. We can even run DNA on it. I've done it before." We might as well do it, though it's really overkill. We have plenty of evidence tying Adams to Truman.

Flory gathers it in, and I ask him to go down to the Tara Foundation when we're done to take a sample of Truman's hair. I don't think he considers this the highlight of his forensic career. I'll call Willie and tell him to expect Flory's arrival.

We go through the clothes in the dresser drawers, and under Adams's socks there is a cell phone. It appears to have been hidden there, though I don't know why Adams would have worried that his room would be searched. Halitzky said that they provide weekly maid service, so maybe Adams was making sure the maid didn't take it.

After Flory dusts the phone for prints, I examine it. Unfortunately, it is locked and requires a fingerprint to open it. "I can't see what's on here," I say to Laurie.

Sam overhears my saying this. "What's the problem?"

"I can't open this," I say. "It requires a fingerprint of the owner. I'm assuming that is Adams."

"Let me see it," he says, and when I give it to him, he adds, "It's an iPhone 6."

"So?"

"So there are ways." He asks Flory, "Can you get me a copy of Adams's thumbprint?"

"Assuming there is one here, of course," Flory says.

I tell Sam that I've read somewhere that you can't just use a copy of a print, that it requires the actual finger. He says something about a high-resolution copy and a dental mold. I have no idea what he's talking about, but I trust Sam in all matters like this.

I tell Sam to work with Jamieson on making sure that whatever he does preserves the integrity of the evidence. But certainly it is crucial that we get into this cell phone; there could be a wealth of information in it.

At the very least it should tell us who Adams talked to and will help us track his movements through the GPS, although it is obvious on its face that he didn't carry this phone at all times. When he left this apartment on the day he died, the phone was in his sock drawer.

When we leave, Laurie and I stop off at Halitzky's office. I thank him for his help and ask, "How much rent was Adams paying?"

"Four hundred a week."

I nod. "Okay, I'll pay his back rent and take the apartment for another four weeks from now. But I want it to stay locked, and I don't want maid service."

"No problem. You can have it as long as you like."

I give him a check for the full amount, and Laurie and I leave. All we can do now is wait for the fingerprint, dog hair, and, most important, Sam's cracking the iPhone that we found. Unfortunately, he says that it could take a while.

I'm not a big fan of waiting.

"They didn't take any film," Hike says.

I don't know what he's talking about, but I'm assuming it's bad news because Hike is the one saying it. Hike could make "you won the lottery" sound ominous and foreboding.

"Who? What film?"

"We got more discovery on James Haley's possessions. We had thought that they might have taken the film that he had been shooting, because the camera was empty. But they didn't; it wasn't there."

"Do they know where it is? Could he have sent it somewhere?"

He shakes his head. "No. And it's not actually film; he shot in digital. But it's all missing. I don't know if he shipped it somewhere, but I doubt it. There were no shipping receipts in his possessions."

"He still could have," I say. "Maybe he has an editor somewhere."

Hike nods. "He does; it was included in the information that Sam found on Haley. His name is Cal Kimes; he lives in Cleveland."

"Can we get him in here? Tell him we'll pay for his flight, put him up in Manhattan, and get him tickets to a show."

Hike shakes his head. "Nothing but junk on Broadway now. All one hundred percent crap."

"When was the last time you saw a Broadway show?"

"Maybe ten years ago. The one where the guy in the mask hangs out in an opera house bothering people. Put me to sleep."

"So you haven't gone in ten years, but you know all the new stuff is one hundred percent crap?" I ask.

"Yeah, that's why I don't go. I remember when Broadway was Broadway."

My only goal in conversations with Hike is to reach the end, and so far I'm not making much progress. "Hike, let's try and get Kimes here, but leave out the part about the shows being crap and Broadway not being Broadway. If he won't come, you're going to have to go out there."

"Then I'll make sure he comes," Hike says, and heads to his office to make some calls.

Like everything else, the missing film, or digital thing, or whatever, could be significant or could be meaningless. Maybe we'll find out when we talk to Kimes, but in the meantime, it changes my perspective.

Until now I haven't given too much thought to motive. I have not yet made any connection between Adams and Haley except for Truman, but that is after the fact. I don't know why Adams would have wanted Haley dead.

I've thought that maybe Haley was shooting some film that presented a danger to someone, and since he was shooting in downtown Paterson, I assumed that "someone" might have been Chico Simmons. But there is also no connection that I am aware of between Adams and Chico, or anyone else in Paterson.

Chico is a gang leader and killer. If he wanted someone in Paterson dead, he wouldn't call Fat Tony Longo in Philadelphia and ask him to send a hit man. He would grab Haley, paint an "X" on his forehead, and put a bullet in it.

I believe that Adams came here from Philadelphia to kill Haley. He did so simultaneously with Haley starting to shoot footage in Paterson, so his motive must have been set before that. Maybe Haley had a

Philadelphia connection; that is something we are going to have to find out.

But how did Joey Gamble get stuck in the middle of this? How would Adams have known that he was a candidate to set up? That's where Chico, or someone like him, would come in. But I just don't see how. It's not like Adams advertised for a framing candidate on Craigslist and Chico answered the ad.

Added to all this confusion is the murder of Denise Adams. As the wife of a mobster, it's fairly safe to assume that her murder was rooted in his world. It also seems likely, though not certain, that her murder was somehow connected to her husband being out of town. Of course, that doesn't mean it was tied to Haley. Maybe she was having an affair with another dangerous guy, and Adams being away gave them an opportunity to be together. And then they had a falling out, and . . .

But Haley, as near as we can tell, was not a part of that world. He was a documentary filmmaker, and not even a major player in that field. To attract someone like Adams, in effect to be worthy of being killed, must have meant he was a danger to someone: Adams, or maybe Fat Tony Longo.

Which means that, at some point, Little

Andy Carpenter and Fat Tony Longo might have to get together.

That will give me something to look forward to.

Cal Kimes clearly does not share Hike's opinion of the Broadway landscape.

He was on a plane hours after Hike called, and Hike met him at Newark Airport. Hike's bringing him to my office, which means that Kimes will have to spend at least forty-five minutes alone in a car with Hike. With that kind of torture, he might jump out of the moving car onto Route 80, or confess to the murder himself.

We've got him staying at the Michelangelo Hotel on Fifty-first Street, which is convenient to his theater tickets. Unfortunately, he wanted to see *Hamilton,* and for the price of the ticket, I could have bought something with bucket seats.

Kimes seems to look around the office with some surprise when Hike brings him in. I think he felt this was going to be a glamorous trip, but my office says the opposite. Hike also walked him through the fruit stand downstairs, which is not exactly the red carpet treatment.

I introduce myself and thank him for coming. "Hey, no problem," he says. "I was really upset to hear about Jimmy."

It's the first time I've heard Haley referred to as anything other than James. It somehow humanizes him, which shouldn't have been necessary. I'm annoyed at myself for thinking of a murder victim as a piece in a puzzle.

"You knew him well?" I ask.

"Pretty well. I mean, we weren't buddies or anything like that, but we worked together. I edited his films, all except for the first one, I think. Maybe the first two."

"He was a talented filmmaker?"

He shrugs. "I guess. I mean, it's a struggle, you know? Everything is low budget. So he did what he could. If he'd had more money to work with, then we would have learned more about how good he was. But here's the thing about Jimmy. He thought of himself as a journalist; he wanted to tell real stories, and he wanted good to come out of it. We could use more people like him . . . and now we have one less."

"How did it work? Did he send you the film as he shot it?"

"He worked in digital," he said. "Has for at least five, six years."

166

"Right, digital. Did he send you the, what do you call it, the digital stuff? Did he send it to you as he shot it?"

"Sometimes he'd send me a hard drive, but not always, and not lately. There was no rush on most of these things, so there was no reason to send me dailies. When the project was done, he'd send me everything. Or usually bring it to me, so we could talk about it, you know, spend some time before we started the editing process."

"Did he send you anything in the days leading up to his death?" I ask.

"No, maybe a year ago, maybe ten months, he changed the way we operated. He did all of the shooting, and then he'd get it to me and we were going to work on it together."

"What was it about?"

"Some kind of diving thing. He was down in Florida."

"Did he mention anything about shooting in the inner city?"

"No. But that doesn't really mean anything; he didn't have to check in with me. And he knew I worked with other filmmakers as well, so I was fine with waiting on him. I figured he'd come to me when he was ready."

"So there was nothing unusual about him

lately that you were aware of?"

He thinks for a moment. "Just that he must have thought one of his films was going to hit big. Last time we talked, he made some comment about how we were going to have the money to do the kind of films we want to make. Money's always an issue in the documentary world."

"Did he say how he would get the money?"

"No. And I didn't ask."

"Why?"

"I guess I didn't believe him. I mean, a movie about diving? Or the one before that, about a drought? One's got water, one has no water. Who cares? And who's going to pay to see it?"

So far I haven't gotten anything worth the cost of the *Hamilton* ticket, but I take another shot. "Help me out on this," I say. "When he shot the footage, where did it go . . . into, like, a digital cassette in the camera?" I'm a dinosaur about stuff like this, but there's no sense in trying to conceal that fact from him.

He half nods. "It's a memory card, maybe this big." He holds his fingers slightly apart to show how small it is. "Then he downloads it into his computer."

"Can he reuse that card?"

"Yes. He just erases it through the computer or in the camera itself. That's called formatting."

I nod. "Okay. So now the footage is on his computer. How does he protect it from a computer crash, or fire, or if he loses it?"

"Backs it up on his external hard drive."

"So all of the footage Haley had just over the past months, where would it be?"

"On his computer and the external hard drive."

"And where would those things be?"

He laughs. "Wherever he is. He would literally never let them out of his sight. I would assume his will said that his computer should be buried with him."

This is very interesting to me. There was no computer or hard drive found in his house after the murder; neither shows up anywhere in the discovery. "Last question," I say. "He shot footage the day he was killed, but no trace of it was found in his house. Nor were his computer or hard drive found."

"Whoa," Kimes says, taken aback. "Only one thing could have happened. Someone stole it." Then, "You think that's why he was killed?"

"Do you?" I ask.

"I don't know. What could have been in

that footage worth killing someone for?"

"Damn good question," I say. "Enjoy *Hamilton.*"

The missing digital footage is something we need to follow up on.

It's not that we have any evidence that it contained something dangerous to someone; it's more that we have no other idea as to why James Haley might have been a target. So we have to investigate whether George Adams, or whoever hired him, was worried about what Haley had on film, or tape, or digital, or whatever.

If we go to trial on this, I'm going to have to learn about this tech stuff. Back in the day, when film was film and Broadway was Broadway, these things used to be easier.

Since we don't have access to the missing video, the best we can do now is try to retrace Haley's steps, to learn where he filmed and when he filmed there.

There are two possible ways for us to do this. One is to put Sam Willis on the case, by supplying Sam with Haley's cell phone number. As he has done a number of times in the past, Sam could use his hacking skills to get into the phone company computer, which allows him to trace the GPS records of the phone. That way we can tell where Haley's phone was at all times. It doesn't mean that Haley was carrying his phone at those times, but it's a good bet that he was.

The other, easier approach to this is fortunately also available to us in this case. The police have already traced Haley's movement in the days after he arrived in Paterson, and the details are properly included in the discovery.

So we'll follow the road map that the police have laid out for us. I'll also put Sam on the case, just in case the police reports have left things out. But I doubt that they did, since their goal would have been to place Haley and Gamble in the same location.

They have been at least partially successful at that, getting some witness statements from people who claim they saw Haley and Gamble in the same place and, in a couple of cases, conversing. It's nothing terribly damaging to us, since we are not claiming they had no contact. For instance, we are clearly admitting to the fact that Gamble's fingerprints were in Haley's house.

Laurie and I are going to retrace the steps Haley took together. I want to do it because the more I can do that is hands-on, the better feel I have for what took place. Laurie will come along not only because she is a professional investigator, but also because we will be going to areas where people might not be so glad to see us.

Laurie sees herself as my protector, which means she sees me as in need of protection. I see her as correct, but I would never admit it to her. I've only recently been willing to admit it to myself.

So off we go into downtown Paterson. Our first stop is Eastside High School, which happens to be where I went to school. Eastside is on Market Street and is generally considered a "tough" school with a history. The movie *Lean on Me,* starring Morgan Freeman, chronicled the controversial efforts of school principal Joe Clark to instill discipline in the place, and the film was actually shot here.

The land that Eastside is on was a cemetery in the 1800s. That is why Eastside's sports teams are nicknamed "the Ghosts." So I went from being a Ghost to being a Violet.

School is not in session, so there are not many people around. According to the records, Haley did some interviews with kids on the basketball courts, but the ones we ask disclaim any knowledge of it and make it clear that they would rather play basketball than talk to us.

The next two stops, farther into downtown, similarly yield nothing. It's obvious that it's much more important to know who Haley talked to and filmed, rather than where he did it.

At a few of our stops, we are looked at warily by youngish males, maybe twenty years old. A bunch of them wear jackets with the letter *X* emblazoned on the back, which I can only assume means they are members of the gang Chico Simmons commands. Joey Gamble's alleged friend Archie Sandler is one of them, but he does not in any way acknowledge knowing us. Nor does he wear the X-marked jacket.

At one point, two of the jacketed ones walk over to us and one of them says, ominously, "What do you want down here?"

It takes me a few moments to pull my tongue out of my throat, so in the interim Laurie says, "That really doesn't concern you."

"Be careful who you're talking to," he says. "You could find yourself in deep shit."

"Be careful who you're threatening," she

174

says. "Now get lost."

I'm sure that they have no idea she is an ex-cop with a loaded gun at the ready, but they don't push it. Instead they laugh derisively and walk away, no doubt to report to their boss.

"I guess we showed them," I say, displaying my pathetic inability to admit embarrassment.

"I think your boy Archie told them who we were. And within seconds their boss Chico is going to know we were here."

I don't say so, but the knowledge of that makes me nervous.

Laurie, not so much.

I'm afraid there is not much to learn here. If Haley had chosen Paterson as a likely venue for his film about urban blight, then he picked the right neighborhoods in Paterson to shoot. Unfortunately, if he found anything dangerous to anyone, especially Adams, it's hard to see what that could be.

The last stop we make today, on Chambers Street, is a puzzling one. It's a funeral home, but there is no indication in the discovery as to why Haley might have been here.

There's no service being held now, so we go into the funeral director's office. We loosely tell the receptionist why we are there; I make a vague reference to police business, which draws a small frown from Laurie. I need to talk to her; if she's going to work with me, she needs to stop being hung up on this honesty thing.

The director is a woman called Linda Markman, who smiles when she welcomes us in. She almost seems happy to see us; she's either lonely or finds it a relief to talk to someone who hasn't just had a death in the family.

I tell her about our trying to retrace Haley's steps, without being specific as to why.

"I definitely remember him," she says. "Nice man." My sense is that she has no idea that Haley became a murder victim soon after being here; I guess she didn't get to host the service.

"Why was he here?" Laurie asks.

"He was making a movie of some kind; something about life in the city. I guess he was showing that death was a part of life. I really didn't ask; I didn't feel like it was my business."

"Was there a funeral here that day?" I ask. She nods. "Oh, yes. That poor man."

"Which poor man was that?"

"Mr. Tolbert. He was killed and his body left in Nash Park in Clifton."

I think that might be the murder Jack Rubin mentioned, but I'm not sure. I turn to Laurie, and she is nodding. "Did he film the service?" I ask.

"No," Markman says. "I couldn't give him permission. I didn't have permission from the family, and I think privacy is important in these matters."

"Do you have contact information for the family?" Laurie asks.

"It was just a cousin, I believe. I did see Mr. Haley talking to him after the service, but he was not filming."

Markman is a bit leery about giving us the cousin's name, and if it was just me I don't think I'd have a prayer of getting it. Fortunately Laurie has a trait that I don't seem to have — I think it's called humanity — and she manages to get it.

Once we're in the car, I ask Laurie if she was in fact familiar with the Tolbert murder.

"Yes. Andy, I think you'd be a lot more familiar with current events if you didn't watch *The Andy Griffith Show* in the morning."

"Laurie, I think you'd be a lot more familiar with modern investigative techniques if you spent some time watching Barney Fife."

"This doesn't make it into coincidence territory," I say. "Not yet, anyway."

"You mean the fact that our murder victim went to the funeral of another murder victim a week before he was killed?" Laurie asks.

"I admit, when you put it like that, it sounds connected. But the guy found in Nash Park was homeless. Even before he was killed, he was a perfectly likely candidate to be profiled in a film about urban blight. Add to that the fact that he was murdered, and he could be the star of the damn film."

"Agreed. But you do think it's worth talking to the cousin, right?"

"Absolutely. More important, you think we're going to run into any issues with Chico Simmons after our little run-in with his buddies?"

"Probably not, unless we start shaking the

tree. But it wouldn't hurt to be careful."

"Maybe I'm missing something," I say. "But do we at this point have any reason to believe that Joey Gamble was an enemy of Chico Simmons?"

"No. Joey's afraid of him, and he's kept his distance, but unless he's hiding something, there's no feud or rivalry."

I nod. "Right. Gamble is a street guy. Maybe not a member of their gang, but on some level one of them."

"So?"

"We're helping Gamble, and we're on the opposite side of their actual enemy, the police. So why are they taking that attitude toward us? Maybe they have no reason to help us, but why would they be opposed to what we're doing? Why would they try to scare us off?"

"We're outsiders," she says. "Don't give them too much credit. We're intruding on their turf and we represent the system. I wouldn't think that they spend much time and effort distinguishing between the various groups in that system. As far as Gamble goes, I doubt that he's important to them either way."

Laurie might be right, but I don't think so. We were not doing anything threatening and yet they tried to scare us off. It may have had nothing to do with us, but rather some secret they are protecting.

I say this to Laurie and add, "Maybe Haley threatened the same secret, and that's why he wound up dead."

"I think that's unlikely," she says, "because that doesn't account for Adams. He's a Philadelphia hood; we have not come up with a reason for him to be worried about a secret on the streets of Paterson. Yet he's the one who wound up with Truman."

She had just identified the problem, the inconsistency, that we keep banging our head against. If Adams hadn't taken Truman, then we'd be thinking Chico Simmons and his gang might be the ones who killed Haley and set up Gamble to take the focus off themselves. That would make sense; it would all seem to fit neatly into place.

But Adams did take Truman; if he hadn't, we wouldn't be stuck in this case in the first place.

I drop Laurie off at home. She's going to contact Tolbert's cousin, while I head down to the jail to see Joey Gamble. I haven't been there in a while, which I feel bad about. I'm basically Joey's only hope, and I don't like for him, or any clients in this position, to think he has been abandoned. So basically I show up to let my clients know that I'm paying attention.

"I thought you forgot about me," is the first thing he says when he's brought into the visiting room. The statement confirms my view and exacerbates my guilt.

"Trust me on something," I say. "My taking your case means I am working on it all the time. No other clients, no other diversions, nothing."

He nods. "Okay. I'm just freaking out a little bit."

"I understand. Now, tell me about Archie Sandler."

"What about him?"

"Do you trust him? Does he have your back?"

He thinks for a moment. "Archie has his own back. It's not his fault; that's the way you have to be on the street. So he probably considers me his friend, and he wouldn't go out of his way to hurt me. But he'll protect himself first; I'd do it the same way."

"Got it."

"Why do you ask?"

I describe to him what happened when Laurie and I ventured into what I assume is the X gang's turf, and how we believe that Archie may have told the gang members who we were.

He nods his understanding. "That would

be Archie's way of getting in good with them, to show he can be depended on. But you should not go down there, and definitely don't bring your girlfriend."

"My wife. My investigator."

"Doesn't matter. Don't bring her; those guys are rough, and they don't give a shit who they hurt."

"Laurie is tougher than I am."

"Hey, I probably got nieces who are tougher than you are. I'm just telling you to be careful."

Why does no one respect my physical prowess? "Hey, if I run into one of your nieces on the street, she's backing down, believe me."

He smiles. "What about my grandmother?"

I shake my head. "I'm not messing with your grandmother."

His smile morphs into a really good laugh, the first one I've seen. I'm starting to like this guy. "You're a smart guy," he says. "Nobody messes with my grandmother. But . . ."

He stops, so I prompt with, "But what?"

More hesitation, and then he says, "Do you think it's possible she believes I did this?"

"Based on my conversation with her, I

would say no, that's not possible."

He nods. "I hope you're right. I don't think I could live with that."

Willis Senack is Christopher Tolbert's cousin. "Second cousin on my mother's side," is his fuller description.

He was quite willing to come talk to me, and since I was going to be in my office going over discovery documents, that's where we've set this meeting. He works, so he couldn't get here until almost six thirty.

Willis looks to be closing in on sixty, and the dark hairs on his head are losing a pitched battle with the advancing gray army. He seems pleasant enough, and had told Laurie on the phone that he would do whatever he could to help, which obviously included driving up from his home in South Orange.

He didn't think he had much to offer, which would put him on par with pretty much every witness we've interviewed so far. But we live in hope.

"How well did you know Mr. Tolbert?" I ask.

"Not well at all, I'm afraid. I used to see him at family dinners, but the older members, the ones who held it all together, have mostly died off. I really don't see any of the family anymore, which is sort of sad."

"When did you see him last?"

He thinks for a short while. "Six years ago? Maybe seven? At my aunt Thelma's funeral."

"You haven't talked to him since then?"

He shakes his head. "No, we were never close. I mean, I heard things; his life obviously spiraled downward. I wish I had reached out to him; maybe I could have helped."

"What did you hear about him?" I ask.

"That he lost his job and was living on the street, though I don't know where. Poor guy."

"Were there drugs involved?"

He shakes his head. "Not that I heard, but you never know, and I couldn't say for sure."

"Who paid for the funeral service?"

Senack shrugs. "I did. I mean, it wasn't fancy or anything. I'm not loaded. But I thought he deserved it. I mean, no matter what happened to him, he was family, and he mattered."

"Any idea who might have murdered him?" I ask, knowing that he won't.

"No. Sorry. I couldn't begin to guess."

"According to the funeral director, there was a man there who wanted to shoot video of the service, but she wouldn't let him. She thought it would be an invasion of privacy."

"Oh, really? I didn't know that. I wouldn't have had a problem with it. I talked to the guy afterward."

I nod. "So I understand. What was the conversation about?"

"Pretty much the same as this one. He just asked me a bunch of questions about Chris, most of which I couldn't help him on."

"Can you remember any of the questions?"

"When did I see him last . . . was he on drugs . . . really the same things you want to know."

"Did he say why he was interested?" I ask.

"He just said he was doing a film about the inner city and all the problems that could be found there, what life was like, that kind of thing."

"Did he film your interview?"

Senack nods. "He did. He had me sign a release. I didn't see any harm in it, so I signed it. You think I shouldn't have?"

"I don't think it matters one way or the other," I say.

"You have any idea when the film will come out?"

The question makes me realize that Senack doesn't know Haley was himself murdered. He probably is like me and doesn't watch the local news.

I don't see any harm in telling him. "It's not going to come out," I say. "He, Mr. Haley, was murdered not long after your cousin."

Senack is clearly shocked to hear this. "Damn, that's terrible. Are the killings related?"

"Good question," I say. "Someday I hope to run into someone who can answer it."

I say good-bye to Senack and thank him for coming. His visit didn't help me much, or at all, and in fact there is probably no way it could have. The idea that Haley was at Tolbert's service merely to gather material for his film chronicling the difficulty of inner city life makes sense.

Senack leaves and I start to gather up some of the discovery documents to take home with me. As I walk toward the file cabinet, I glance out the window and see Senack leave the building and start walking down the street.

Unfortunately, I also see two young males standing across the street in a doorway, trying not to make it too obvious that they are looking toward the first floor exit of my building.

They are the two guys who threatened Laurie and me on the street . . . the two guys with an X on their jackets.

Shit.

I am not without options here, and if my heart would stop pounding, I could focus on them.

I could go down through the fruit stand and sneak out the back door into the alley. That's not a great idea, in case they have people stationed in that alley. Alley fighting is not a specialty of mine.

Another possibility is to call the police. The problem is that I don't know what they would do when they got here. They can't arrest the guys standing in front of that store; store standing is not a crime.

I could get them to escort me to my car, unless I had really bad luck and they happened to be cops who know me or, worse, cops I've embarrassed on the witness stand. In that case, they'd probably let the gang guys borrow their guns. Either way, while I might escape this immediate problem, it would be delaying the inevitable.

The third option is the one I take, and the one I always take in these situations.

I call Laurie.

Some people tend to babble when they're afraid, but I'm the opposite. I speak clearly and succinctly; I can even stop my teeth from chattering in the process. So in very few words I tell Laurie exactly what is going on.

"They're just standing there?" she asks.

"Yeah. I assume they're waiting for me to come out."

"I'll call you back in sixty seconds," she says, and hangs up. She beats her sixty-second prediction by eight seconds.

"Okay. Marcus is going to call you within fifteen minutes. When he does, go downstairs and out through the front, but make an immediate right turn down into the alley. Then just walk; Marcus will be there."

"What if they have guys stationed in the alley as well?" I realize the question is stupid the moment it leaves my mouth. "Never mind," I say. "Marcus will be there."

"Right," she says. "And I'm on my way."

"You sure we shouldn't call 9-1-1?"

"They're not breaking any laws. And this way maybe we can get some information out of them. But try to keep an eye on them without them seeing you. If they start toward your office before Marcus gets there, call 9-1-1 and lock yourself in the bathroom."

"It's not a vault, Laurie. It's a bathroom."

"Andy, just be careful and protect yourself for the next twelve to fifteen minutes."

She hangs up, and now I am alone. These twelve to fifteen minutes are going to feel like twelve to fifteen months. I go to the window and peek out; the guys are still standing there. I hope they are the patient type.

Marcus beats Laurie's fifteen-minute prediction by one minute and thirty-eight seconds . . . not that I'm counting. His message to me when I answer the phone is a grunt that sounds like "Nwhn."

It could mean anything from "Now" to "No, I'm not coming, I'm home changing diapers." But Laurie said he was coming and he has never not shown up before. I have to think that if he wasn't going to be here, he would have told her that, and she would have called and relayed the message in comprehensible English.

I really hope he's here, especially since I'm going to be walking into the alley alone and unarmed. I feel like Michael Corleone hoping that the gun is actually taped to the bathroom tank so that he can go shoot Sollozzo and Captain McCluskey. But this situation is even worse, because if the gun wasn't there, Michael would still be able to go out and eat the best veal in the city. I'm not going to have that option in the alley.

But if I'm going to do this, I have to do it right, so I turn out the lights in the office to alert the bad guys that I am, in fact, leaving. It's important that they notice.

I go downstairs, stopping to take a quick look out the back window to see if they have any buddies waiting back there. I don't see anyone, but I don't have a sightline to the whole area.

Finally I open the front door. It's gotten pretty dark out, and while there is a streetlight not too far away, the area where I am is not very well lit. I don't want to look toward the bad guys, but I do want to make sure they see me. So I pause for a few moments, almost as if I'm deciding which direction to go in.

Then I close the door pretty hard behind me. I don't slam it, because that might be too obvious, but it should be loud enough for them to hear it, if they haven't already seen me.

I've left enough clues about my departure for anyone with half a brain to follow, but in the brief conversation Laurie and I had with them the other day, I got the feeling that neither had ever been offered a Rhodes Scholarship.

So now all that is left for me to do is either go into the alley or lie on the ground and curl up in the fetal position.

I go into the alley.

It's pretty dark here in the alley. There's some light from the building next door, but not much.

I peer ahead as I walk, but I don't see Marcus. The buildings have some columns that jut out into the alley, and he could be behind one of them; it's hard to see in the dark. Of course, no one ever sees Marcus until Marcus wants to be seen. Sometimes I think he can beam himself in and out of places at will.

I hear noises behind me. Those noises sound like feet walking quickly. While I don't turn around, I have a strong feeling that the people who own those feet are wearing jackets with an X on the back.

I increase my pace slightly, resisting simultaneous urges to break into a run and scream "Marcus!" The walking noises behind me seem quicker, closer, scarier.

Then there is a different noise, sort of a

muffled combination scream, gasp, and moan. Now I do turn around, and in the dim light, I see three people. One of them is lying on the ground, motionless. Another is being thrown against the side of the building by the third figure, who I sure as hell hope is Marcus.

It's a weird visual. He throws the guy against the wall from about three feet away, and the guy bounces back to him. Then he throws him again. It's a form of handball, except the ball is human . . . and moaning.

I walk back toward them and say, "Marcus."

He turns to me and stops the wall-bouncing routine. Instead he pushes the guy forward, toward me and the end of the alley. Then he reaches down, grabs the collar of the guy who seems to be out cold, and starts dragging him along. The only sound is coming from the guy's shoes, as the backs scrape along the cement.

So I fall in as well, and we make a weird procession to the back of the building. It's a bit lighter back here, and I see something I hadn't noticed before. There's a third potential assailant, also lying unconscious on the ground. At least I hope that's his condition; it's pretty hard to tell the difference between unconscious and dead in a dark alley, from a distance.

Marcus has been busy.

We stop near the third guy and Marcus deposits the unconscious guy he has been dragging next to him. His head comes to rest on the third guy's chest; under different circumstances it would be sort of a poignant scene. In this case it is scary and surreal, and for the life of me I cannot remember a law school class in which this scenario was covered.

Marcus makes a motion that seems to indicate that I have the floor.

"What's your name?" I ask the one who's still conscious.

He doesn't answer, so I ask again. He continues not to answer, so Marcus takes a threatening half step toward him. "They call me Zip."

"I don't care what they call you. What's your name?"

"Alex."

"Alex what?" I ask.

"Huh?" he asks in return.

My interrogation has obviously got a great flow going, which is mercifully interrupted when Laurie comes walking down the alley toward us.

"Everyone okay?" she asks.

"Only on the good-guy team," I say.

"What have we learned so far?"

"The conscious one's name is Alex, but they call him Zip." There is some moaning coming from the two guys on the ground, but I'm still keeping them in the "unconscious" category.

I turn my attention back toward Zip. "Why were you coming after me?"

"We weren't coming after you."

"Zip, don't disappoint me."

"We were just going to scare you," he says.

"Better men than you have tried," I say. "Who sent you?"

"Nobody."

"Was it Chico Simmons?"

"Don't know him."

Marcus starts to take another step toward him, but Laurie holds up her hand, and he stops. "Maybe I can get somewhere with him. Zip, come down here with me. We need to talk."

She starts to walk down the alley, taking Zip by the arm and moving him along. "Be careful," I say.

Laurie holds up her left hand, which has her handgun in it. "Zip and I will be fine."

So Laurie and Zip walk down the alley and engage in a conversation that I cannot hear, but which goes on for at least five minutes.

Alone time with Marcus always makes me uncomfortable, and the presence of two groggy gang members does nothing to ease that feeling. I say, "Thank you," to Marcus, since he once again saved me, and he responds with a grunt of some sort. I guess I could be making small talk, maybe asking how the baby is doing, but this doesn't really feel like the appropriate time or place.

Laurie and Zip finally come back toward us. When they arrive, Laurie says, "Zip and his friends are free to go, as soon as they are able. We can leave now."

Obviously Laurie doesn't want to speak in front of the three defeated assailants, so I don't ask her what was said. I trust her instincts just to go along, and I know she will be updating me as soon as possible.

As we start to walk away, Laurie says, "Let's go for a cup of coffee."

We drive to a diner on Route 4 in Elmwood Park.

There's no sense hanging around in my office neighborhood, in case Chico Simmons sends out a posse to look for Zip and friends. Because Laurie, Marcus, and I all came in separate cars, we don't get a chance to talk until we're all situated in a booth in the back of the diner.

The place is relatively empty, so we can talk without fear of being overheard. Which is good, because I am dying to hear what Laurie has to say.

The waitress comes over and Laurie and I order coffee. Marcus orders a club sandwich, a hamburger, clam chowder, and pasta. I have never seen anyone eat like Marcus, but I resist the temptation to ask the waitress to bring him a shovel.

"I think I'd like to hear about you and Zip now," I say, when the waitress finally leaves to get a flatbed trailer on which to bring Marcus his food.

Laurie nods. "Okay. At first Zip didn't want to say anything. So I threatened him. I told him that Marcus was going to drive away with him, just the two of them. That scared him, no question about that, yet he still wouldn't answer my questions in any meaningful way."

"I hope we're approaching a 'but,' " I say.

"We are. But when that threat didn't work, I told him that we were going to have the police pick up Chico Simmons for questioning for murder, and have them mention that it was Zip who fingered him. That scared the hell out of him, so he said he would talk as long as it didn't get back to anyone, meaning Chico."

"He was more scared of Chico than of Marcus?" I ask. I, for one, would be more scared of Marcus than of Jack the Ripper. Or Godzilla. Or Russia. When Laurie nods, I add, "Chico must be a very unpleasant guy."

"No doubt," she says. Marcus has no comment; he's in the process of inhaling the entire basket of bread. Laurie continues, "But even though Zip was suddenly willing to talk, he really had nothing to say regarding our case. He'd never heard of Haley and had no idea why we were asking about him."

"You believed him?"

"At first I didn't, but then I did. Zip thought we were there because of a different murder."

"What does that mean? What murder is that?"

"Christopher Tolbert, the homeless guy found executed in Nash Park. The guy whose funeral service Haley attended."

"I don't understand," I say, because I don't. "What did Zip have to do with that?"

"He claims he had nothing to do with it, which may or may not be true. But reading between the lines, he basically said that Chico was behind it."

"What did Tolbert have to do with Chico?"

"Zip doesn't know, or at least he claims he doesn't know. But I couldn't get any more out of him. I told him that if we find out he's lying, Marcus would pay him a visit, and that we would spread the word that he fingered Chico. You could call it double jeopardy. But I couldn't get anything else; I don't think there was anything to get."

When Marcus eventually finishes eating, we get the check. Laurie and I each only had coffee, and the bill comes to sixty-one dollars. But based on Marcus's efforts tonight, it is without a doubt the best sixty-one dollars I've ever spent.

Laurie and I obviously drive home separately. I get there first, and when I open the door, Tara is standing there with her leash in her mouth; it is her way of telling me I'm home later than promised. Sebastian is asleep in his bed, which is his default position.

I doubt that Tara will care if I offer excuses about Zip and Marcus, so instead I take both of them outside. Laurie pulls up and joins me on the walk.

"What do you make of what Zip told me?" she asks.

"I'm not sure yet; I need some time to process it. I assumed that Haley went to that funeral service strictly because of the film he was shooting; it made sense that he might do that. But he questioned Joey Gamble about Chico, and now he goes to a service for a murder victim that Chico is tied to. The coincidence alarm is going off."

"There's something linking Chico to Adams to Haley to Tolbert," she says. "And while I don't know what it is, it sure as hell has nothing to do with Joey Gamble, who is sitting in jail."

"Let's talk this through, because I'm feeling like all the players here have been other than what they appeared to be. Maybe the same is true for Tolbert."

"How so?"

"Well, he was homeless and on the street, so we just accepted that he was in the wrong place at the wrong time, and got himself killed. But he was executed; he wasn't beaten to death by punks on the street. And he apparently had nothing of value, so robbery wasn't a motive.

"There's something else I was thinking about on the ride home. When I spoke to your friend Sergeant Rubin in Philadelphia, he originally thought we might be calling about the Tolbert murder. I hadn't even heard about it at that point, but he said that they had two murders that fit the same MO. He even thought they might have a serial killer on their hands."

"So you think they might be connected?"

I nod. "All along we couldn't understand where Adams fit in; I mean, what the hell brought him here from Philadelphia? But if he's the link, then maybe it starts to fit."

"So let's find out what we can about Tolbert," she says. "I'll call Rubin to try to get more information about the Philadelphia cases."

"Unfortunately, we won't have standing to get discovery information on Tolbert because we can't connect it to our case.

What Zip told you in an alley would not be compelling to the court, and Dylan won't give it to us if he doesn't have to."

"So you want to put Sam on it? Maybe he can find something about Tolbert online that we don't know."

"It's worth a shot," I say. "At this point, pretty much everything is worth a shot."

Laurie is going to have Marcus watch out for me.

I know that for a couple of reasons. One is that whenever I'm in any kind of danger, she has Marcus watch out for me. The other is that she just said, "I told Marcus to watch out for you."

I could argue the point, but she won't give in and I'll just look weak when I cave. Trying not to look weak is particularly important to weak people like myself; it's one of our weaknesses.

Instead I just say, "Not today. Please tell me it's not starting today." We're on our way to Ricky's camp for visiting day, and the last thing I want is Marcus hovering around the ten-year-olds. It could easily send them to therapy until they are visiting their own grandchildren at camp fifty years from now.

"No, it wasn't necessary to start today,"

she says. I know she means that she is here to protect me today, so Marcus doesn't have to. It's one humiliation after another.

I never went to overnight camp when I was a kid. We weren't poor by any means, but that was an extravagance that was a bit beyond our means. I was always fine with that and have remained fine until today.

The camp is a really cool place. Great sports facilities, a beautiful lake for swimming, a building chock-full of computers and other techie stuff . . . what's not to like?

Seeing Ricky is phenomenal. All the parents waited down near the ballfield when the kids came running down. Ricky came at full speed to us and gave us both big hugs; he seemed genuinely happy to see us. And we could not have been happier to see him.

So we've spent the day letting him take us around the camp, showing us the projects that he's worked on, demonstrating his newfound ability to swim, and introducing us to his friends. He clearly loves being here, and I love that he loves being here.

I just wish he would come home with us.

But the day is not ending on a high note. There is a father-son foul-shot tournament in the gym. Through a very unfortunate series of flukes, the two finalists are Ricky from the kids, and me from the fathers. And at this moment, I am about to shoot for the final time.

If I make it, the fathers and I win. If I miss it, the sons and Ricky win.

I don't know what to do, and Laurie is too far away among the observers in the stands to give me advice. I don't want to win; I want Ricky to win. But while the easy thing to do would be to intentionally miss, I have this vague feeling that it would be wrong to do so. It feels somehow dishonorable and worthy of Ricky's disapproval, even though he would never know.

But making it feels even worse. Why shouldn't the kids win? Wouldn't that make everybody happy, including all the parents? And wouldn't they look at me with justified disapproval if I beat all their kids, including my own?

So I'm going to miss, without making it too obvious. I'll shoot it to the right, clanging it off the rim and letting it fall harmlessly to the floor. Then I'll pretend to be disappointed, but, good loser that I am, I will proudly put Ricky on my shoulders and let him bask in his victory. And every parent in the place will know I missed on purpose and will think I am terrific for having done so.

Losing is a win-win.

I am not a very good shooter, and though I aim to the right, I miss my target by three inches, to the left. That sends the ball swishing smoothly through the net and means that this visiting day will forever be known as the day Andy Carpenter made losers out of a bunch of ten-year-olds.

Once we're in the car and heading home, Laurie says, "You tried to miss that shot."

It isn't a question, just a statement, so there is no need to deny it. She knows me too well anyway. "I did," I say. "I missed the miss. I choked under pressure. You think Ricky will get over it?"

"I think he forgot it already," she says. "He's having way too much fun to let something like that bother him."

"That's the difference between us," I say. "It will bother me for the rest of my life."

We're still a couple of hours from home when my cell phone rings, and I see by the caller ID that it's Sam Willis. "Hey, Sam," is my clever opening.

"Andy, are you still at the camp?"

"On the way home."

"You have fun?" he asks.

"I hit the game-winning shot," I say, as Laurie looks over at me and frowns.

"Cool. Ricky must have been proud."

"He was thrilled. What's up?"

"It's about the Tolbert case."

We had given Sam the task of finding out what he could about Tolbert, hoping to uncover something to connect him to Haley and our case. I had also told him about the similar cases in Philadelphia, in case he could dig up some connection there too.

"What about it?" I ask.

"I've got something to show you. Can I bring it over when you get home?"

I'm not happy to get this request; I'm tired and I want to walk the dogs when I get home and go to sleep early. Destroying a bunch of ten-year-olds' sports dreams is exhausting. "Can it wait until tomorrow?"

"It can; actually, that will give me more time to search and put it all together."

"What is it?"

"Andy, I think it's better that you see it. Then you'll be in a better position to make a judgment on it."

"Okay, Sam. Come by the house in the morning?"

"You got it, Chief."

Trial dates remind me of cars in the passenger-side mirror.

They don't actually move, but they are closer, and I mean always closer, than they appear. And the one constant is that defense attorneys are never ready for them. You could tell me that a trial is scheduled for twelve years from Tuesday, and I'd be cramming at the last minute and complaining that I need more time.

Today marks a shift in preparation for me, and one I probably should have made a while ago. Until now we've been focused on the investigative phase, mostly trying to figure out who actually committed the murder, since our obvious position is that our client did not. Clearly we think it's Adams, so we've been trying to find proof of that theory.

But it won't be long before the prosecution is parading a group of witnesses in front of the jury, all of whom will tell a story incriminating Joey Gamble. We need to prepare a defense to rebut those witnesses. Defense is what defense attorneys like me are supposed to do.

In this trial, the simplicity of the prosecution's case will make a defense that much harder to mount. Dylan is not going to rely on witnesses whom I could challenge to make it appear that they are lying or mistaken.

Joey's fingerprints were all over Haley's house, and the stolen merchandise and murder weapon were found on Joey's property. Those are facts that can't be challenged on credibility grounds. All we can do is try to explain them, try to give them a benign meaning, which is a very tall order.

Laurie makes pancakes for breakfast this morning, because if Sam is coming over, he's coming for breakfast. Sam is Marcus-like when it comes to his ability to eat pancakes, and Laurie's are his favorites. Or so he says.

Sure enough, Sam is right on time. He's brought a large folder full of material, but I tell him to eat first. Otherwise he might drool all over the papers.

Eleven pancakes later, we're sitting in the den as Sam starts to unload the folder. "I don't know what to make of this," Sam says. "I sort of couldn't believe it as I was doing it."

"Any luck with Adams's phone?" Laurie asks. Sam has been trying to get through the fingerprint identification problem on Adams's iPhone.

He shakes his head. "No. He had another level of protection installed on it. But I'm getting there."

I'm sure that if it can be done, Sam will do it, so I don't press him. "So you said this is about Tolbert?"

"In a way. At least, that's where it started out. You remember you asked me to check into him, to find out what I could, in case there was more to him than meets the eye? I was looking for something that would have made him a logical candidate for someone to want to kill him."

I nod. "Right. Did you find anything?"

"No. You also told me about the Philadelphia killings and wanted to see if I could find a connection between Tolbert and them."

Sam has a way of recounting past history as a way of setting the scene for his revelations. It can turn a five-minute conversation into an hour-long marathon. "Sam, I know what we asked you to do. Did you find the connection?"

"No."

"Well, now we're getting someplace."

Laurie jumps in. "What did you want to show us, Sam?"

"I'm getting there. You know I can get into a lot of computer databases, and in some cases law enforcement ones."

"I know, but I don't want to know," I say.

He nods. "I understand. Well, I didn't do that in this case. I can, and it might turn up a lot more, but so far I haven't."

I think I am going to bang my head against the wall until Sam stops dragging this out. "Sam . . ."

"So I was just using a bunch of different search terms, you know, describing the victims, the murder, the type of killing, that kind of stuff. I was searching for information about Tolbert and also the Philadelphia homeless victims."

"Good," Laurie says. I think she's getting frustrated too; she just hides it better.

"Here's the thing," Sam says. "I started finding other cases, all within the last six months, that have the same or a very similar set of facts." He looks at the papers. "So when I found some, I started looking for more. So far I've discovered a total of eighteen."

"Eighteen murders?"

He nods. "Not including the three you know about."

"Where?"

"All over. All fairly large cities, urban areas, where you would expect to find a homeless problem. But LA, Chicago, Dallas, Atlanta, you name it."

"Take us through them," I say.

So Sam goes through them, one by one, and it certainly seems remarkable. Now, I am sure that homeless people are often victimized, but this has to be over the top.

"If you want me to go into law enforcement computers, I might be able to eliminate some of these cases with more detailed information," Sam says. "But I bet you I find a bunch that we don't even know about."

"Don't, Sam, at least for now. Let us sit with this awhile and figure out what to do. But you did great work. Now go back and crack Adams's phone."

Once Sam leaves, Laurie quickly makes it clear that she finds this information as stunning as I do. But it's a big country; maybe this is just more generally common than we think?

Laurie calls Sergeant Rubin in Philadelphia to see if there have been any developments in the Denise Adams murder. She puts me on the other phone so I can hear his responses. "Not my case," he says. "But I don't think so. I would have heard."

"What about the killings of the two homeless people?"

"Now you're interested in *that*?" he asks.

"Laurie has a murder fascination," I say. "She's trying to deal with it in therapy."

He laughs. "Well, sorry to disappoint, but nothing new on that front either."

We don't want to reveal too much to him, at least not right now, so she asks him in general terms about homeless murders and whether it is a widespread problem around the country. He says he's sure it must be, but by his answer we can tell that what might have happened in other cities is not yet part of his case. He doesn't know what we know; that much is clear.

"Time to call Cindy," Laurie says.

"I think we should wait and see if this can impact our case," I say, since my first allegiance has to be to my client.

"Andy, people are dying."

I nod. "You're right. Time to call Cindy."

Cindy Spodek is the second in command of the Boston FBI office.

That is not why we are calling her; it will come as no surprise to hear that there are closer FBI offices to Paterson. We are calling her because she is a very close friend of Laurie's and, by the principle of marital extension, mine.

This won't be the first time we have gone to the "favor well," and in the past Cindy has helped us a great deal. It's often worked out to her benefit, but that's sort of not the point. I call her when I need help. She knows that, of course, and usually gives me a hard time. Laurie, being Laurie, mediates, and we get through it.

But this time is different, as I tell Cindy when Laurie puts me on the phone. Laurie always does a little "friend talk" first, smoothing the way for me to swoop in and ask the favor. "What do you need, Andy?"

Cindy asks, a note of resignation in her voice.

"You think I'm calling for a favor?"

"Of course. This is Andy Carpenter, right?"

"You're probably not going to believe it, but I'm actually calling to do you a favor. This is something you need to hear."

She sighs, obviously not convinced. "Fine, let's hear it."

"No, you should see it as well as hear it. I need to come up there."

"Excuse me? This is actually not you looking for help on a case?"

"It's possible, but that's a long shot. This is something else," I say.

"Okay, come on up. When do you want to meet?"

"Tonight. I'll take you to dinner and show you."

"So this is really that important?" she asks.

"This is very important. Or not important at all. But you have the resources to make that judgment. I don't."

"Are there conditions attached to this?

"Of course," I say. "But nothing terrible. I'll tell you about it when I see you."

"I'll make a reservation someplace quiet and very, very expensive," she says.

It's about a four-hour drive to Boston,

which means it's much faster to drive than to take a thirty-five-minute flight, after you factor in going to the airport, getting through security, renting a car, etc., etc., etc. And that's assuming the flights are on time, which, from a New York airport, is as likely as the Mets winning the World Series. In four games.

Of course, the three hours assumes no traffic, which is an absolute impossibility. I've done this drive at least ten times, and every time I hit traffic in Connecticut. Connecticut? Why would there be so many people on the road in Connecticut? Are they going to a Yale game? Or maybe they're on their way to Muffy and Buffy's for watercress sandwiches?

So the drive takes four and a half hours, meaning I don't even have time to check in at the hotel before going to the restaurant Cindy has chosen, Mamma Maria. It's in the North End, in a nineteenth-century townhouse, which indicates that Cindy is going to deliver on her promise of "expensive." There aren't too many Taco Bells set in nineteenth-century townhouses.

I assume Marcus is also here, watching over me, but very often he likes to remain unseen, even by me. I'm fine with that.

I'm brought to a private room where

Cindy is waiting for me. The server closes the door behind me, leaving Cindy and me alone. Privacy is not going to be a problem.

We make small talk for a bit and look at the menus. At first I'm worried when I see things like "snail" and "rabbit," but then I see more normal stuff at surprisingly reasonable prices. I order a salad and a lobster pasta. Cindy gets crab cakes and the same pasta.

Finally, she says, "Talk to me. I'm intrigued."

"Okay, but first a short preamble." I have no intention of discussing my case with her. It's not just because there is attorney-client privilege involved; it's also because I have found that in my dealings with the Bureau, information is the currency of the realm.

I might want to trade what I know later on; there is no reason for me to give it away now. "My preamble basically consists of setting up a quid pro quo," I say.

She smiles. "You never travel without your quid pro quo."

"How true. So I'm about to give you the reason for this lovely dinner. In return, should you find it compelling and worthy of an FBI investigation, you will keep me as updated as you can about its progress. Especially about anything that relates to my client's case."

"I don't know anything about your client's case."

"That's a fair point. You just give me the information and I'll judge if it's relevant."

"I'll keep you updated to the extent that I can," she says. It's the answer I expected and the only one she could have given. It's good enough for me because it is Cindy who has said it; if it were one of her colleagues, I might feel differently about it.

"Fair enough. There's a Philadelphia gangster named George Adams, who has recently become a dead Philadelphia gangster. He is connected to my case, so I talked to a Philadelphia cop to get background on him.

"During that conversation, the cop mentioned that there were two recent homicides of homeless men being investigated. The circumstances were nearly exactly like those of a case that we had in Clifton. A homeless man named Christopher Tolbert was killed, execution-style."

"Okay . . ." she prompts, which is FBI-ese for "Tell me more."

"In all three cases, gunshot wounds were the cause of death, and there was no evidence of drugs in the toxicological tests."

"So you think there's a connection? And

220

you're here because it's taken place across two states and is therefore federal?"

"You're getting warm," I say. "Our investigator, using only publicly available records, news stories, etc. has identified eighteen additional cases that match the original three almost exactly."

"Holy shit," she says. "Where?"

"All across the country. You might be able to find a lot more of them, should you choose to look."

"I will choose to look," she says.

"Good. What's for dessert?"

The good news is that Sam has cracked Adams's phone.

The bad news is obvious the moment he says, "There's not much here, Andy."

I'm in Sam's office, which is right down the hall from mine, where he has all the information in hard copy, laid out on his desk. It's not a good sign that it takes up barely half the desk.

"He just didn't use this phone much," Sam says. "There are only eighteen phone calls in the two months before he died, and eleven of them were to his house. He was probably calling his wife."

"What about the others?"

He shrugs. "All to numbers in Philadelphia. I've got the names listed there," he says, pointing to one of the papers on the desk, "but they don't mean anything to me. Two of them are to a restaurant; for all I know he was picking up take-out."

"What else have you got?"

"Not much. The guy didn't even use apps; no music, no Words with Friends, nothing."

"Maybe he had another phone, which might be why he didn't have this one with him when he died."

"But why would he have hidden this one in that drawer?" Sam asks. "There's nothing incriminating on it."

"Add that to the list of questions," I say. "What about GPS? Can you find out where the phone has been?" Smartphones are equipped with a GPS, and the phone company knows where they are at all times; they can even access the information retroactively.

Sam has broken into the phone company's computers for us and retrieved similar information on a number of occasions; I have found it to be both illegal and very helpful, not necessarily in that order.

He looks at me with disdain; I expect him to say "Duh." Instead he says, "Of course I did that already. Mostly stuff around Philadelphia. I checked as best I could but didn't see much. Nothing near the murder scenes of the homeless victims, but I don't know that they were killed where they were found."

"Does it show when he came up here?"

He nods. "Yes, and —"

I interrupt. "That might clear him of his wife's murder. You were going to say something?"

"Yes. He seems to have stopped at a motel near East Brunswick."

"To stay overnight? Or a bathroom break?"

"He didn't stay overnight, and if it was a bathroom break, he had a really bad stomach. He stayed four hours, then he drove the rest of the way up here."

"You have the name and address of the motel?"

"Of course."

"You want to take a ride? Did you bring your shoe leather?"

"Absolutely."

Before we go, I call Laurie and tell her what's going on and where we're going. I know Marcus is watching out for me, and whether I like it or not, he'll be doing it when we go to the motel. He might as well know where we're going.

"Do you think Marcus would want to ride with us?' I ask this with some level of dread. An hour-long drive with Marcus is a conversational wasteland, even with Sam in the car.

"No, he can do his job better watching

you rather than being with you," she says.

"Damn. I was so looking forward to chatting with him."

So Sam and I head down to the Bay View Motel in East Brunswick. The name is somewhat misleading. It's not anywhere near a bay, and although it does have a view, that view seems to be of a Chinese restaurant and a laundromat.

It's serviceable — not a dump, but also not a particularly nice place. I don't know why Adams stopped here, but it seems as if the main things it has going for it are that it would guarantee some anonymity and has a fairly close proximity to the turnpike.

The motel itself looks to have about sixty rooms on two levels, all with outside access. In fact, that is the only access; guests park their cars near their rooms and either walk in from the parking lot or go up the steps to the second floor. I don't see any signs of an elevator.

We drive quickly around the parking lot, checking the place out, and then head for the office. I ask the man behind the desk for the manager and he says, "You're talking to him."

I introduce myself and Sam, and the man says his name is Peter Ambler. "Friends call me Pete," he says, which doesn't really speak to much creativity on the part of his friends.

"Pete, we're interested in someone who was here a while back."

"Why?"

I explain that I am an attorney and that the matter is relevant to a case currently before the court. I imply rather strongly that if he doesn't willingly yield to my charm and answer my questions, he just might have to explain his refusal to the judge.

That empty threat seems to work, so I show him a picture of George Adams, but if there's a flash of recognition in his eyes, he's hiding it well.

"When was he here?" he asks, and I tell him. "But he was only here for about four hours."

That information seems to perk him up a bit. "When did you say it was?" he asks, and I give him the date again.

"That might be the guy," he says. He goes over to his computer and starts typing. "I think that's him. But the name he used was Charlie Henderson."

Charlie Henderson is the name Adams used when he turned Truman in and when he rented his apartment, so it's obvious we have the right guy.

"You remember him?"

He shakes his head. "I don't, but I know my wife does."

"He met your wife?" I ask.

"She does the housekeeping . . . cleans the rooms . . . makes the beds." He shrugs. "It's a family business."

"And she remembers him? Is she working today? Is she here?"

"She's home, but I'm sure she'd come by. We live right next door." Another shrug. "It cuts down on the commute."

I ask Ambler to call her, and sure enough, within five minutes Peggy Ambler shows up at the office. She continues the family propensity for wild nicknames by telling us that people call her "Peg."

She's a pleasant woman with a nice smile, but there is a toughness in her face that comes through. She's also no more than five foot two and would weigh a hundred pounds if she were holding barbells in both hands.

She looks like a person who does what is necessary and is not afraid of hard work. Which must be the case, because she's cleaning up to sixty rooms a day. I find that hard to identify with; when Laurie is out of town, I would rather set fire to our bed than make it.

Pete does the introductions and shows the

picture to Peg. "That's him," she says.

"You're sure he was here?"

"Oh, yeah. He creeped me out. There was an air about him like he was dangerous. If he stayed overnight, I was going to ask Pete to make up his room."

"Did he say anything to you?" I ask.

"No, he kept the 'Do Not Disturb' sign on the door. That was fine with me. And the other guy was even creepier."

"What other guy?"

She shrugs. "I don't know his name or anything, but there was something off about him. He was only here for about twenty minutes."

"Did you talk to him?"

"I was making up the rooms in that section. He was looking around like he didn't know where he was going, so I asked if I could help him. He didn't say anything; it was like he looked through me, like I wasn't there. It gives me a chill just to think about that guy."

"What did he look like?"

"I'd say about six foot, maybe a little bigger, black hair, like, these full eyebrows, and his mouth was a little bent, like on a very slight tilt."

"You have a good memory," I say.

"The guy was scary; it was just the way he

carried himself."

"If we had a sketch artist come, do you think you could describe him well enough for a picture to be drawn?"

"I don't know . . . I doubt it. I've never tried something like that, and I only saw him briefly."

"Anything else you can tell us?"

She thinks for a moment, then says, "No, he showed up and wasn't here long. I remember telling Pete that they couldn't have been up to any good, and . . . but I did hear him say something when he left."

"What was it?"

"He said, 'Just do what you're told.' It sounded like a threat; I even expected him to add 'or else,' but he didn't. I think the guy in the room answered him, but I couldn't hear what he said. I'm sorry I can't remember any more."

"Peg, you're actually amazing."

As a general rule, law enforcement investigations move slowly.

There are exceptions, of course, but that is usually when the answers being sought are obvious and the clues readily apparent.

I feel like we are surrounded by slow-moving — and, in some cases, stalled — investigations. To my knowledge, the Philly cops are getting nowhere on the Denise Adams killing, while our local cops are having a similar lack of success on both the Christopher Tolbert and George Adams homicides.

I also haven't heard a word in more than a week from Cindy Spodek, who is trying to discover whether there is a link between the homeless murders that Sam discovered across the country. I have to admit that I'm getting pissed off at her unresponsiveness; I either have given her a monster case or a sack of nothing, and it shouldn't take her that long to figure out which it is.

And of course hovering over all of this is the fact that our own investigation, the one that we're conducting in defense of our client, is getting nowhere fast.

So this morning I am doing what I like to do when I am under stress but have some free time during a trial: I'm at the Tara Foundation hanging out with the dogs. Dogs relax me; they help me think. They don't argue with me, they don't object when I say something in court, and they don't pound their gavel when I'm being obnoxious.

I bring Tara with me; she loves hanging out with new friends, and there is fortunately a lot of turnover at the Foundation. Whenever we place a dog in a home, it opens up a spot to bring a new one in. Tara hasn't been here in a couple of weeks, so there are a whole bunch of dogs she hasn't met yet.

Sebastian didn't come with us. He doesn't like to socialize much; it interferes with his sleep. Pretty much the only thing Sebastian allows to keep him awake is food; if he could find a way to eat in his sleep, he'd be in heaven.

Willie is out getting supplies, which in this case means hundreds of pounds of kibble, dog toys, and Pill Pockets, a tasty treat that masks the pills we put inside. A lot of dogs that we rescue, who almost by definition didn't have great treatment and medical care before they were abandoned, have ailments that we have to deal with. Willie and Sondra give out more medicine than Walgreens.

Sondra is completely capable of handling things on her own, but Willie will make sure to be back by ten o'clock. That's when potential adopters start showing up, by appointment, and no one leaves here with a dog without Willie signing off on it. These dogs are his children, and he makes sure that any home they go to is a damn good one.

"How's Truman?" I ask.

Sondra smiles. "Doing great now, but he was a handful at first. He follows Willie everywhere. We've been taking him home at night and he's sleeping on our bed. It just takes him a while to trust people." She laughs. "He and Willie are a lot alike in that way."

Then she says, "Check this out." She takes out her phone and shows me a picture of Willie asleep in their bed. Truman is on the bed as well, sleeping with his head on Willie's chest.

Once Sondra has her phone out, she feels the need to show me what seems like hundreds of pictures of other dogs, many of whom are here at the foundation now. I'm looking at them live, so I'm not sure why I need to see photos.

But I don't complain, because taking pictures is Sondra's thing; I just have no idea why she wants them all, whether she looks at them, or where she keeps them.

"Where do you keep all these pictures? Does your phone have enough room?"

"I usually keep them for a month or two," she says, "and then I store them on the Cloud. I also ask people who adopt the dogs to send me pictures of them in their new homes. So the pictures add up."

The whole idea of the Cloud bewilders me. Like with most tech things, I don't have a current need to know. My fear is that there will come a point where life is not possible without learning this stuff. "Must be nice having your own Cloud," I say.

She smiles. "It belongs to everyone, Andy. Including you."

She's right; the Cloud belongs to everyone. Why didn't I think of that before? I call Sam and ask, "When you looked at Adams's phone, did you check to see if he had anything stored on the Cloud? Is it even possible to do that?"

"Holy shit, Andy. I'm an idiot. It never entered my mind."

"Can you do it?"

"Of course. The tough part was getting into the phone. Where are you?"

"At the foundation."

"I'll get back to you. Damn, I'm stupid."

Clearly Sam is stunned by my coming up with a possible tech solution he hadn't; I don't think I'll mention the fact that it was Sondra who was behind it, and that I wouldn't recognize the Cloud if I were flying through it. "Sam, don't be so hard on yourself. You're not stupid; you're just not as technologically savvy as I am. Very few people are."

Willie gets back and I help him carry the supplies into the foundation building. The first potential adopters show up, a couple in their thirties. They're here to meet and potentially adopt a shepherd mix named Roger, and they all go into the adoption room with Willie.

I don't go in with them. I have full confidence that if they want Roger, Willie will make the correct decision on whether they will treat him in the way he deserves. Also, on the chance he turns them down, I don't want to be a part of that conversation. Willie can be blunt; confrontation avoidance, one of my specialties as long as I'm outside the courtroom, is not on his list of personality traits.

They come out about a half hour later, and it's clear that it didn't work out. I can tell that from their body language: the husband seems defeated and the wife seems angry. Also, the fact that Roger is not with them is a significant hint.

"No good?" I ask Willie after they leave.

"Not even close. They have a doghouse in the backyard, but if the weather is bad, then Roger could come in and stay in the basement."

"Oh."

"But the asshole husband said Roger would be a member of the family. Do they keep their kids in the backyard or the basement? I should have taken the guy apart."

"I think you showed admirable restraint," I say.

"Yeah. But I still should have messed him up."

I'd better leave before Willie messes the next guy up. But as I'm about to, Sam shows up, carrying his briefcase. "You were right," he says. "It was on the Cloud."

"What was?"

"Take a look; I printed it out." The first

paper he takes out of his briefcase is a photograph of a man who sort of reminds me of Peggy Ambler's description of the man who visited George Adams at the motel. He's a big guy with dark hair and thick eyebrows, though if his mouth has a tilt, I don't see it. He also has a closely cropped beard, which Peggy did not mention.

Sam takes more pages out; they are newspaper stories about the guy, who is named Frank Silvio. He appears to be a mobster out of Florida, based in Miami, and there are stories of his violence written in a way that makes him seem legendary.

"Can you find out more about this guy? He could be the one Peggy Ambler described," I say.

"I will, but it can't be him," Sam says.

"Why not?"

"Because he's been dead for six months."

I ask Sam to go home, scan Silvio's photograph, and send it to Peggy Ambler.

Obviously I want to know if she identifies him as the man who visited George Adams at the motel. It will be puzzling if that's the case, since he was dead at the time.

But I guess stranger things have happened.

Sam calls me fifteen minutes after he sends her the photo, while I'm on my way home. "She's not sure. She says it could be him, but the beard is throwing her."

I ask him to email the photo and the newspaper clippings to Cindy Spodek and then I call Laurie. I quickly tell her what is going on and ask her to call Cindy and tell her the photo is coming.

I instinctively feel that this is very important, and not just because he may have met with Adams. Adams could have met with a lot of people having nothing to do with our case. But here the meeting was shortly before Adams killed James Haley; our view is that he was literally on his way north to do just that.

Maybe even more significant is the fact that Adams apparently took pains to learn about the mysterious visitor; he downloaded his photo and newspaper stories about him. And then, in the most revealing action of all, he erased it all from his phone and hid it in the Cloud.

When I get home, I call Cindy and ask if she received the material.

"Just did," she says. "I don't know anything about him, other than what the news stories say."

"That's disappointing," I say.

"Sorry, I am not familiar with every bad guy in the country; but I'll see what I can find out."

"Great. Still nothing on that other matter? You know, the one where people are dying all over the country?" I'm not great at hiding my annoyance, a trait that some people find annoying.

"Relax, Andy. Nothing definitive, but we're getting there," she says.

"Let me know when you're all the way there. That was our deal."

"I'm aware of our deal, Andy. Keep in

mind that I'm just the number two person in the Boston FBI office. I'm not the director, or the attorney general. There are decisions that I don't make, and there is information that I am not given."

"This has made its way to the director and attorney general?"

"I don't know where it has made its way, Andy. I was making a point about my place on the Justice Department totem pole."

She promises to find out what she can about Silvio, which doesn't exactly make me euphoric. Dealing with the government, even when that government is a friend, can be slow and ponderous. With the trial close to starting, slow and ponderous really doesn't work for me.

Sam Willis, on the other hand, is the exact opposite. He brings over an entire dossier on Silvio, built from online sources and official documents, including some from various courts. I don't ask Sam how he got the court documents because I don't want to know the answer.

All of it paints a picture of Silvio as a career criminal, though not one successfully dealt with by the justice system. He seems to have been based in Florida, more specifically in Tampa. But while he has been arrested four times for violent crimes, none of the charges have gone to trial, and two of those arrests took place in other states. Silvio got around and spread the violent wealth.

He died in a boating accident almost seven months ago off the west coast of Florida north of Tampa. He was alone on the boat as a storm came in. He sent out an SOS, but by the time the local maritime people got to his boat, he'd gone overboard, and his body was never found.

I don't know how they determined he was dead, and I'm suspicious of it. When it comes to bad guys, I don't believe they're dead until I've watched their body lowered into the ground, and even then I have my doubts. Missing bodies just don't cut it, especially when it's entirely possible that this missing body recently spent twenty minutes in an East Brunswick motel with George Adams.

"You need to go to Florida," Laurie says.

"I'll send Hike," I say, feeling guilty for doing that to Florida.

"It should be you," Laurie says. When I frown, she adds, "You know I'm right."

"Ricky is coming home from camp this weekend."

She nods. "That's why I'm not going with you. But it is very likely that Silvio has something to do with this case, whether or not that was him meeting with Adams at the motel. The point is that Adams was researching him and hiding it in the Cloud."

"I don't want to let Ricky down," I say, starting to grasp at straws.

"He'll understand. And besides, he probably hates you because of the foul-shooting contest."

"Thanks a lot."

"Let me get you someone to meet with down there."

"What does that mean?"

She doesn't answer and instead just goes to the phone. What follows is a remarkable demonstration of the game of "law enforcement telephone," one in which my role is strictly that of admiring observer.

Laurie calls Sergeant Ben Ammons, an ex-colleague of hers on the force who was the union rep and attended various conventions with other officers from around the country.

He does not know anyone in the area of Florida where Silvio died, but thinks that Lieutenant Gary Aguilar in Atlanta might, because he thinks Aguilar was originally from Miami.

Aguilar sends Laurie on to Sergeant Terry Burgess in Miami, who knows a cop in

Tarpon Springs, Florida, named Lieutenant John Hunnicutt. Tarpon Springs is within a few miles of the area in question.

Laurie then calls Hunnicutt, tells him that Terry Burgess suggested she call, and fills him in on our story. He says he's happy to help, so Laurie says that I will be in his office tomorrow afternoon.

It's an amazing performance; if I ever tried to play the attorney version of that game, it would take three weeks and I'd have to keep signing a bunch of release forms. And I'd wind up with an ambulance chaser two hundred miles from where I wanted to be.

After all of that, there is no way I can get out of going. "I'll book the flights."

"For two," she says. "Marcus is going with you."

"Oh, no."

"Andy, you have already been threatened and almost attacked."

"That was by Chico Simmons. He's local."

"We don't know who is who, or where is where. But we do know that we are dealing with dangerous people. Marcus is going with you, so book the flights for two."

"Yes, ma'am. Should I order him a kosher meal?"

The flight isn't as awful as I expected.

Marcus has his headphones on the whole way, listening to classical music. You haven't lived until you've seen Marcus Clark's feet tapping to the strains of Vivaldi.

All in all, it could have been much worse: the plane wasn't delayed, it didn't crash, and I'm not traveling with Hike.

We land at the Tampa airport and I rent a car for the twenty-seven-mile drive to Tarpon Springs, where Lieutenant Hunnicutt is supposed to be available to us. It is oppressively hot, close to a hundred degrees, and makes New Jersey feel like Juneau.

Marcus rents his own car; Laurie told me that was what he was going to do. I assume not being with me, but rather being able to watch from a distance, makes it easier to protect me. That's fine with me; I have a number of goals for this trip, but living through it is at the top of the list.

The drive to Tarpon Springs takes about forty-five minutes. It is a small seaside town that seems to exist because of its proximity to the water. Everything seems to be huddled toward the coast, and if there is ever a national boat shortage, it won't be because of Tarpon Springs.

I go straight to the hotel where Laurie made reservations. It's a Hampton Inn, which is fine. I prefer modern hotels with elevators, flat-screen televisions, room service, and wireless to inns with quaintness and character. And since I'm traveling with Marcus, romantic isn't that important either.

I check in to both rooms, and when I go back out to my car, there is Marcus, parked next to me. I give him the key to his room and then drive off; I assume he'll follow me, but I don't know that for sure. At this point I'm not feeling in any particular danger.

I go to the Tarpon Springs police station, and sure enough, I'm brought right in to see Lieutenant Hunnicutt. His looks defines the phrase "grizzled veteran"; he's in great physical shape but has got to be nearing retirement age. He has clearly spent a lot of his life in the Florida sun; his face has the texture of the first baseman's mitt I used in high school.

But he greets me with a relaxed smile, and I thank him for taking the time. He shrugs it off, saying, "Any friend of Terry Burgess . . ."

It takes me a few seconds to realize that Burgess is the Miami cop who put Laurie in touch with Hunnicutt. He must think I know Burgess personally, so I just say, "That Terry is quite a guy."

"She's a woman," he says.

I nod. "But as tough a cop as any guy I know."

He frowns slightly, but doesn't seem to view gender misidentification as a reason to end the conversation. "So what do you want to know?"

"I'm not completely sure; it's one of those cases where I won't know until I know. But it centers on two main areas. One, a guy by the name of James Haley came down here and shot some footage for a documentary. I need someone who can give me a road map as to where he went, what he shot, and who he spoke to."

"And Haley is not available to help you with that?"

"He was murdered not long after being here."

He nods. "What's the other area you are interested in?"

"Frank Silvio."

He almost does a double take; he is obviously very familiar with Frank Silvio. "He's dead."

"Are you sure?" I ask.

"I didn't see the body, if that's what you mean. And it obviously didn't happen here, so I wasn't involved, but he was identified through DNA."

"Let's start at the beginning, if that's okay," I say. I ask him to describe the area in general terms and Wilton Key, the town where Silvio was killed, more specifically.

"Tarpon Springs, where we're sitting right now, has long been the center of the sponge-diving industry. Greek people settled here and started it in the early nineteen hundreds, and we still have the largest Greek population in the country. Don't leave here without trying the baklava. The sponge industry is still strong, and it's at least partially responsible for a good tourist turnout as well.

"Other smaller towns have sprung up along the coast near here as well; they're just small municipalities that are basically miniature versions of Tarpon Springs, minus the Greeks. They survive on sponge diving and tourism."

"And Wilton Key is one of them?"

"It is. One of five."

"The filmmaker I mentioned, James Haley, did some shooting in Miranda City."

He nods. "It's the next town over from Wilton. They share some facilities and services; police, fire . . . that kind of stuff. Each town on its own is too small to handle it. Sorry, but I'm not familiar with Haley. Unless he got in some trouble here, I wouldn't be."

"And what can you tell me about Silvio?"

"A seriously bad guy. Originally out of Miami, the crime family he was a part of expanded into Tampa. He was the main enforcer, and I mean that in the worst sense of the word."

"He was head of the family?"

"No, that honor fell to Anthony Mazzante. Silvio was easily his most valued employee; he was said to have been like a son to Mazzante. But then Mazzante got himself throat cancer and pretty soon went to that great crime family in the sky. And even though Silvio was like a son to him, Mazzante had a real son who took over the family. It was convenient; Mazzante's son is also named Anthony, so they didn't have to change the towels."

"And the younger Anthony wasn't quite as crazy about Silvio?"

"Apparently not; I guess it was a sibling rivalry of sorts," he says. "But that was just the rumor; I have no firsthand knowledge of it. And now it doesn't really matter."

"So the younger Mazzante had Silvio removed from the picture?"

"Hard to say. But Silvio owned a boat, a thirty-five-footer. He took it out a lot; he was an experienced seaman. Apparently it relaxed him between killings. So on this particular late afternoon, he is said to have gone out on it alone, despite the fact that there was a storm predicted. It didn't work out so well."

"But the body was never recovered?"

"No, but there was DNA evidence. You might want to talk to the local cops there; I don't have all the details."

"Can you set it up for me?"

He smiles. "Sure, any friend of Terry Burgess . . ."

I return the smile. "Quite a woman, that Terry."

Before I go back to the hotel, I take a drive to Miranda City, the town where James Haley shot the trailer about sponge diving that I saw online. It's a very small town with everything centered on the pier. Across the street are a few restaurants and bars, plus some buildings where tourists can sign up for sponge-diving expeditions.

I go into one of the bars; it's fairly crowded, which surprises me, because the street outside is mostly empty. None of the patrons have the look of tourists; this is a local place. It also has an intimidating feel, although that could just be me. People look over at me when I walk in, but it's not like anybody brandishes a knife or makes throat-cutting gestures.

A large group of people are near the television set, watching the Tampa Bay Ray's game. That would be reason itself not to move here. The other reason would be the Buccaneers; this is not exactly a sports mecca.

The bartender sees me and comes over. "What can I get you?"

I almost say "information," but that sounds too much like a bad old movie. Instead I ask for a light beer, which draws a bit of a frown along with a nod. I don't think this is a "light beer" kind of place.

When he brings the beer, I say, "Have you ever seen this guy?" and show him a photo of James Haley. I try to speak and show the photo so the other people at the bar can't see or hear what's going on, but that is pretty much impossible. Fortunately, as far as I can tell, no one is interested.

"Who wants to know?" the bartender asks. Based on that line, I think he's seen the same bad old movie.

"I do. My name is Andy Carpenter; I'm a private detective." It's not that big a lie. I actually am private, in that I value my privacy. I admit the "detective" part is a stretch, but it's not like I'm under oath.

"I don't know him," he says. I have a feeling he would have said that had I shown him a picture of his own brother.

There's a woman sitting about three feet away from me at the bar, and I sense that she is interested and trying to see the photograph as I show it to the bartender.

I hold it up for her. "Have you ever seen him?"

She just shakes her head and turns away without saying a word. It is the same reaction I have gotten many times from women in bars over the years.

I turn back to the bartender. "What about Frank Silvio? What do you know about him?"

"Drink your beer," he says, and walks away. The woman next to me also walks away, leaving the bar entirely. I'm making a lot of friends here.

So I drink my beer, watch an inning of the Rays game, and head back to the Hampton Inn. Just another night of life in the Andy Carpenter fast lane.

I have no idea where Marcus is.

He's seen only when he wants to be seen. I know the right thing to do would be to call him and ask where he is and if he wants to have dinner, but I can't seem to get myself to do it.

I want to go to my room, order room service, and get some sleep. I'm tired, I don't want to be here, I don't want to have a client and an upcoming trial, and I don't want to have to be protected from gang guys and who knows what else.

Other than that, I'm feeling upbeat and in a good mood.

Hunnicutt has gotten me a morning meeting with Sergeant Mike Morrison, head of the four-person police department that covers the groups of small towns of which Wilton Key and Miranda City are part. I'm not sure what I'll learn, if anything, but at least

I got to spend some quality time with Marcus.

I call home to make sure that Ricky got home from camp okay. Laurie and the other parents were meeting the bus in Englewood. I'm feeling very guilty and a bit resentful that I wasn't there to greet him.

But just hearing Laurie's voice makes me feel better. She sounds really happy; I know she was missing Ricky at least as much as I was. He's playing in his room with his best friend, Will Rubenstein; they're having a sleepover, which means they spend the night doing anything but sleeping. When Laurie tells him I'm on the phone, he comes running.

"Hey, Dad! Where are you?"

"I'm in Florida."

"When you coming home?"

"Very soon, Rick. I can't wait to see you."

I ask him a bunch of questions about the last week of camp, color war, the bus ride home . . . whatever I ask him about, he pronounces as "great." He doesn't even seem bitter about the foul-shooting contest; I guess it will be up to a therapist to bring that out in future sessions.

Laurie gets back on the phone and our talk goes to the kind of chitchat reserved for loving couples: we discuss the various murders we are dealing with.

She's more hopeful than I am that we'll come up with something. "It's there to be found, Andy. Adams wasn't hiding that stuff in the Cloud because he was in the Frank Silvio fan club."

"Maybe. But you realize how many other possibilities there could be? James Haley was not George Adams's first rodeo; he spent a career doing bad stuff. Silvio could have been involved in any one of those other things; we have no evidence that he had anything to do with our case.

"In fact, if he really is dead, a death which apparently has been confirmed by DNA evidence, then he could not have been involved with our case. For all we know, Adams could have been the one to kill Silvio; maybe that's why he was carrying Silvio's picture around. Maybe he wanted to make sure he killed the right guy."

I continue my soliloquy. "And to make matters worse, I ordered a club sandwich without mayonnaise from room service, and they brought it dripping with mayonnaise. It is impossible to get a club sandwich without mayonnaise in this country. It was a hell of a lot different in the old days; they respected condiment preference back then. And Broadway was Broadway."

"You finished venting?" she asks.

"No, I ordered the french fries crisp and . . . yeah, I'm finished."

"Then what does your gut tell you?"

"That it hates mayonnaise."

"Andy . . ."

"Okay. My gut tells me that there is something down here to be found. At its core our case is about the victim, James Haley, and the guy we believe murdered him, George Adams. Haley was down here shooting footage, then went north and was murdered. Adams was tied in to Silvio, who went missing down here.

"This is not that large an area; the fact that all aspects of our case connect to it has got to mean something."

Laurie agrees with me, but then also adds a logical question: "But let's say we're right about this. Where does Chico Simmons fit in? And why was James Haley at Christopher Tolbert's funeral?"

"Maybe the two things are completely unrelated," I say.

"How so?"

"Well, we're thinking it's all connected, all part of the same puzzle. Maybe the situation in Paterson is a separate issue. Maybe Chico was just annoyed that Haley was filming on his turf — trespassing, as it were.

And maybe Haley just went to Tolbert's funeral because he was a homeless guy on the street who got killed. What better example of urban blight could there be than that?"

"That's possible," she allows.

"Maybe Haley was just a really annoying, nosy guy. So he pissed people off down here, and then he went north and pissed off Chico Simmons. But there's a decent chance the two things have nothing to do with each other."

"And what about the other murders that Sam uncovered around the country?"

I try to come up with a logical answer that includes every aspect of the case. If the widespread killings that Sam discovered are in fact unrelated, then it has nothing to do with our case. But if the opposite is true, if they are connected and part of a pattern, then it is beyond my current understanding.

Their connection would mean that it is part of organized crime, in the literal rather than the popular meaning. A large number of powerful people, not to mention dangerous ones, would have gotten together, would have organized, to engineer these deaths.

But why? These were homeless men; what value could they have had to their killers?

They couldn't all have been eccentrics with huge bags of cash tucked away in their non-existent mattresses. And if it wasn't something that they had to take away, could it have been a threat they represented? Could they have had knowledge that made them dangerous?

I don't know any of these answers, so my response to Laurie is, "Beats the shit out of me."

I hang up the phone and turn on the television. I doze off and am awakened by a knock on my door. I don't like knocks on the door when I'm in a strange place; I actually find myself hoping it's Marcus.

I go to the door. "Who is it?"

"Please open the door." It's a woman's voice, speaking softly. I look through the peephole and discover that the reason it's a woman's voice is because it's a woman doing the speaking. And unless I'm mistaken, it's the woman who was standing next to me at the bar, the one who denied having seen James Haley.

She looks scared.

Join the club.

For all I know, there could be someone with her, but I'm counting on the invisible Marcus to make sure that's not the case. I open the door and she doesn't wait for an invitation; she just walks by me and into the room.

"You are going to want to hear what I have to tell you," she says. "I think they killed my Vincent."

"Who is your Vincent, and who do you think killed him?"

She tells me that her name is Lorna Diaz and that Vincent Grobin is, or was, her boyfriend, and she believes that the divers killed him. According to her, Vincent is, or was, one of those divers.

I'm not sure why she's here and talking to me, but I have a feeling that the bar I was asking questions in was not exactly under the cone of silence.

"Which divers are you talking about?" I asked.

"The boat he worked on; it's called the *Ginny May.* There are other divers on the boat; he was afraid of them."

"Why did he continue to work there?"

"He was going to make a lot of money. He was afraid, but he couldn't turn down the money."

This is not getting any clearer to me; nor

do I understand why she came here to tell me about it. "Why don't you tell me the whole story?" I suggest, since my questions are not really getting the job done.

So Lorna starts talking and I keep listening, and it gets more interesting as she continues. Her boyfriend, Vincent, has been promising her for months that they were going to be married and get rich, not necessarily in that order.

He wouldn't tell her how it was going to happen, and she sensed he was fearful about parts of it, but the lure of the money was too great. He even told her when he would get the money: October 5. That was her birthday, she said, and they were going to leave Florida. They were going to leave for California, where apparently they would get married and live happily ever after.

Grobin, according to Lorna, wasn't friends with his coworkers and said they could be dangerous; he scrupulously kept Lorna away from them.

She says that she warned him to be careful and said that money wasn't what was important to her, but he disregarded the warnings. Then one day he went to work and never came back. She went down to the docks and spoke to the others on the boat, but they disclaimed any knowledge of a problem, saying that Vincent had just not shown up for work that day, without calling in.

Lorna is positive that they are lying, that Vincent loves her and would never just disappear without contacting her.

"Did you go to the police?" I ask.

She nods. "They are doing nothing. Divers come and go all the time, they say. Vincent is not from around here, so they said he probably went home. They said they would file a report, but I don't believe them."

"So you don't trust the local police?"

She laughs at the question. "No. No one here does."

I ask what kind of boat Vincent worked on and she says it is a tourist boat. They dive for natural sponges, and retrieve some, but basically they make their money by taking tourists out and letting them observe the diving.

"Were there tourists on the boat the day Vincent disappeared?"

She shakes her head. "They say the boat was being repaired that day and didn't go out. They are lying."

"The photograph I showed you in the bar — have you ever seen that man? Do you know if Vincent ever met him?"

She nods. "Yes; that's why I knew I should come talk to you. He is the man from the movies."

Now we're getting somewhere. "And Vincent spoke to him?"

"Yes, at our house. They spoke alone; I don't know what they talked about." Then, "You're a detective; can you help me find out what happened to Vincent?"

I don't see how I'd be able to help her even if I were a private detective. I don't know whether anyone can help her because I don't know if what she is saying is at all accurate.

I do think that she's telling the truth as she sees it; that's not the issue. Clearly she believes what she is saying, but that doesn't mean it's accurate. Vincent Grobin could have just left town, or somehow cut off all contact with her.

I am suspicious, of course. Just my being down here is evidence of that. I'm especially intrigued by the talk of large amounts of money; it reminds me of Marcus saying that the word was that Chico Simmons suddenly had large amounts of money to spread around. Also, James Haley had told his editor, Cal Kimes, that he was going to get enough money to make the kind of movies that they wanted to.

And now Lorna has set a target date for the resolution of whatever it is to be resolved . . . October 5.

But all of this is a long way from knowing one way or the other whether Grobin was the victim of foul play.

"I don't know how I can help you, but if I can, I will," is the best I can offer her.

She doesn't seem thrilled with my response; the look of disappointment on her face is obvious. I'm a pretty good judge of that; I've been disappointing women since high school.

She gives me her phone number, thanks me, and leaves. I resume watching television, reclining on the bed in a dozing position. It doesn't take long before I am in full doze mode; I vaguely know in the back of my mind that at some point I should wake up, take my clothes off, and get under the covers, but that does not seem like a priority at this point.

Suddenly, annoyingly, there is another knock on the door. This time it's a stronger, more authoritative and demanding knock, and therefore more worrisome. As I get up I look at the clock and see that an hour has passed since Lorna Diaz left.

This time I don't ask who it is; I don't want to reveal that I'm even in the room. I look through the peephole and the good news is that it's not someone there to kill me. The bad news is that it's Marcus.

I open the door.

"Come," he says. "Now."

Lorna Diaz is sitting in the back seat of Marcus's car.

As signs go, this is not a good one, and it's made worse by the obvious fact that she has been crying. She's still sobbing softly as Marcus and I get in the front and pull away from the hotel.

"What happened?" I ask. I'm hoping she is composed enough to answer, because Marcus seems disinclined to.

"I drove home and parked behind my house. Someone in the alley . . . attacked me from behind . . . he was choking me. Then this man . . ." she says, meaning Marcus.

"Marcus," I say. "His name is Marcus. He intervened?" It's a pretty good bet that happened, since Marcus is a world-class intervener. If intervening were an Olympic sport, Marcus would have a boatload of medals.

She nods. "He would have killed me. I

265

couldn't breathe."

"Where is the man now?"

"Behind my house. He's . . . I'm sure he's dead. The side of his head was . . . I'm sure he is dead."

"Is that where we're going now?" The question is addressed to Marcus, even though I know the answer. There's a dead body behind this woman's house, and Marcus is bringing me there.

Marcus nods. I briefly consider jumping out of the car, but it will only be a temporary solution. Instead I put the pieces together. With me tucked safely in my room, Marcus must have seen Lorna leave the hotel and followed her to make sure she was safe.

It was a smart move; she was obviously not safe. She was attacked, probably because she had come to see me. Her attacker must have been afraid that she was revealing knowledge that was dangerous to him, or to those he worked for. Marcus then did what Marcus does, which is why there is a body waiting at the end of this drive.

We arrive at Lorna's house after a brief five-minute drive. She lives in what seems to be a rundown area outside of town, though I've lost my bearings and don't even know which town it is. The body is still there, as predicted. Marcus must have clubbed him in the head with his elbow or forearm; his head looks like it lost a battle with a truck.

"Do you know who he is?" I ask.

"I don't know his name, but he is one of the people who worked with Vincent."

Marcus has obviously brought me here because I am to be the decision maker as to what our next step is. One thing is certain; that next step is going to be all-important.

The question is whether or not we report this to the local police. It doesn't take a lawyer to know that doing so is the proper procedure. A man has died; he was justifiably killed to save the person he was himself trying to kill, but that doesn't change the fact that he is dead.

I know that Marcus acted properly, but in a civilized society that is not my call to make. That is a police and prosecutorial function.

But in a civilized society those same police are supposed to be the good guys, and I have serious doubts that that is the case here. Lorna said that they are corrupt and that everyone living here believes that as well. She also said that Vincent Grobin was murdered, and the events that have transpired since she left my hotel have only bolstered her credibility.

More significantly, I have no doubt that Silvio's death was faked, but I have real doubts that it could have been pulled off without the police being complicit in the setup. So I think there is a good to excellent chance that at least some of the cops here are, in fact, corrupt.

For me, in a situation like this, it always comes down to an upside-downside analysis. Whether we report it or not, the upside is that we don't get hassled and we get to go home without facing any kind of charges. The guy is dead and will remain dead, no matter what we do.

But if we report it, then the potential downside is enormous.

Marcus could wind up in jail.

I simply cannot take that chance.

I call Marcus over to the side and talk softly so that Lorna cannot hear us. "Marcus, we are required to report this to the police, but we are not going to report this to the police."

He doesn't say anything, doesn't nod, doesn't even blink.

"Lorna does not trust the police in this town, and based on what's happened, I'm inclined to trust her opinion about that. If we report it, it could get very ugly for both of us."

Silence from Marcus.

"Can you do something with our friend here so that he is not found, at least not for quite a while?"

He nods.

"Good. Can you drive me back first? I don't want to call a cab; that would establish a record in case anyone gets suspicious as to my whereabouts."

Another nod.

Now I go back to Lorna. "Lorna, it's important that you never speak about this to anyone. It would be very dangerous to you, and could also get Marcus in trouble."

"He saved my life."

"I understand, but it's still dangerous for you to stay here. Is there anywhere you can go? Do you have family anywhere?"

"I have a sister in Atlanta, but I have no money."

I have seven hundred dollars in cash and I give it to her. She doesn't want to take it, but I insist. "Leave tomorrow morning," I say. "There will be a time you can come back, but it won't be for a while."

"And Vincent?" she asks.

"I'm afraid you may have been right about Vincent."

Marcus drives me back to the hotel. I turn on the television and get back into bed, but this time I can't fall asleep for a very long time.

Wilton Key makes Tarpon Springs look like Midtown Manhattan.

It's even smaller than Miranda City, though similar in style. It's a tiny community totally contained within three blocks of the shoreline. I haven't counted, though that would be relatively easy to do, but it seems as if there are as many boats docked here as there are buildings in the town.

Like Tarpon Springs and Miranda City, the dominant industry seems to be sponge fishing. Each place along the harbor appears either to be a working sponge company or a tourist attraction centered on sponge diving. Vacationers can go out on working boats and watch the sponge divers in action; based on the signs the trips are either half day or full day.

The *Ginny May,* the boat Lorna had said was where Vincent worked, is on the north end of the pier, the third boat in. Its sign advertises tourist excursions to observe the "ancient art" of sponge diving.

The boat is sitting there unattended at the moment. It's similar in size and style to the others at the pier; I know nothing about boats, so I have no idea if there are any significant differences. I also don't know if the owners and/or crew have an awareness that one of their colleagues is missing.

The police station, such as it is, is across the street from the pier. It's a small building, barely distinguishable from the shops and offices alongside it. I enter into a reception area maybe ten feet square with a single desk manned by a uniformed officer.

"Can I help you?" he says.

"I'm here to see Mike Morrison . . . Sergeant Morrison." Morrison is the cop Hunnicutt contacted on my behalf.

"He expecting you?"

"I think Lieutenant Hunnicutt from Tarpon Springs told him I'd be by."

He nods and yells out, "Sergeant, someone here to see you."

Sergeant Morrison comes out from the back room, which I believe is the only other room in the building. "Yeah?"

I identify myself and he nods in recognition. "Come on back." When we're settled in the sparse office, he says, "So what's this about?"

"I'm investigating the death of Frank Silvio."

"Why?"

"It's tangentially related to a case I have back home. Can you tell me the circumstances?"

He shrugs. "I can tell you what we know, which isn't much. Witnesses saw him go out on his boat, alone. A storm came in and we got an SOS from the boat. Once we were able to, we went out there and just found wreckage."

"He was experienced out on the water? He knew what he was doing on a boat?"

"Yes. No doubt."

"Wouldn't he have known better than to go out with a storm coming in?"

He shrugs. "Sometimes the fact that guys have a lot of experience makes them think they can handle anything. They become less careful, when it should be the opposite."

"I understand there was DNA evidence?"

He nods. "Bloodstains on a piece of wood, which would have been part of a bench. The theory is that he was thrown and hit his head. No way of knowing whether he went overboard, or went down when the boat broke apart."

"But no body?"

"Wouldn't expect there to be."

"Were you out there when the wreckage was found?"

"No, one of my officers. He does most of the work out on the water when necessary, rescues or whatever."

I don't want to express my doubts that Silvio is really dead, because I have no idea if Sergeant Morrison can be trusted. I'm not about to reveal anything significant to him.

He also seems pretty mellow and shows no signs of stress, so I'm pretty sure he doesn't know Marcus clubbed someone to death last night. "Do you know James Haley?" I ask. "He's a filmmaker who was down here shooting footage for a documentary."

He thinks for a few moments. "Yeah, he stopped in here. Just checking in to tell me what he was doing. Nice guy. Is the movie finished?"

"Not yet," I say, opting also not to share what I know about Haley. I want to ask Morrison about Vincent Grobin, but I don't want to say anything that will tie me to last night's events. My hope is that Lorna Diaz is on the way to her sister's house in Atlanta and that she can begin to put this behind her. Last night must have been shocking and frightening for her. I can say with certainty that it was shocking and frightening for me.

I'm not going to learn anything more from Sergeant Morrison or from wandering around town. I leave and look across the street at the *Ginny May.* There are two crewmen there, but no real activity. Maybe they are waiting for their colleague to find out how last night went. They're going to have a long wait.

This place is giving me the creeps. I take out my cell phone and call Marcus. "Yunh?" he says.

"Let's get the hell out of here," I say.

On the way back to the hotel I call Lieutenant Hunnicutt in Tarpon Springs and tell him that I need to hire an investigator down here.

"Did I give you the impression I was looking to become your HR director?" he asks.

I laugh. "No, but you're a top candidate, and this is your chance to prove yourself." I go on to say that I need somebody good, somebody discreet, and somebody able to meet me at the hotel in forty-five minutes.

"I'll call you back," he says, and he does call back, in five minutes. "Jack Hagans is on his way. He's as good as it gets down here."

Fifteen minutes after we get to the hotel, I get a call saying that Hagans is downstairs. I ask him to come up and am struck by his appearance. Marcus is an investigator, and if he has an exact opposite in the field, at least physically, it's Hagans. He is probably in his fifties, five foot seven and a hundred and forty pounds.

But I'm not hiring him to beat anybody up, and after I talk to him for a few minutes, he seems knowledgeable and smart. He gets $250 an hour, so he obviously doesn't charge by the pound.

I'm not very specific in what I tell him to do. I want him to observe the *Ginny May* and its crew as closely as he can, and report back to me what he learns. He asks what it is I'm looking for and I say that I don't have any idea, but that I think there might be some criminal activity going on.

That seems to work for him, and I ask him to report by telephone every three days. I don't know if anything will come of it, but I do know that if he is down here, then I don't have to be.

That alone makes him worth the money.

The flight home gives me a lot of time to think.

I'm looking forward to telling Laurie the events of the last couple of days and discussing what I think is going on.

When I get home, Laurie, Ricky, Tara, and Sebastian are waiting for me on the porch. Ricky runs down the steps and I lift him in a big hug. Laurie and Tara are not far behind. Sebastian couldn't care less.

I am one lucky guy.

We all take Tara and Sebastian for a walk and then spend another half hour in the den, with Ricky regaling us with camp stories. In honor of my return, Ricky is given the choice of anything he wants for dinner, and he chooses pizza.

That's my boy.

When Ricky finally goes to his room, I tell Laurie everything that's happened down in Florida. She is of course stunned to hear about the attack on Lorna Diaz and Marcus's lethal intervention. I have no doubt that she disagrees with my handling of it; the ex-cop in Laurie would have preferred that we report the entire incident to the police. But she doesn't criticize what we did and realizes the hassles such a report would have caused. And if the police down there are actually corrupt, then it could have gone much further than just mere hassles and inconveniences.

On some level I think she trusts Marcus more than me to deal with these kind of situations. Marcus is unflappable and physical danger doesn't stress him out the way it does me. I doubt Laurie thinks Marcus would have gone along with my plan if he didn't think it was the correct approach.

So she doesn't argue with me or lecture me on the evil of what I have done. It's over, and it's not like I need to learn how to handle these things in the future. The chance that I will have to ponder what to do with a dead body in a back alley will hopefully not come up again, though the way things are going, you never know.

We agree to leave open the possibility of reporting the incident later on, perhaps to Cindy. But I don't make any commitment to do so, and I doubt that I will. The upside-downside analysis will likely still hold.

With that out of the way, Laurie asks me what my impressions are of the situation down there and its effect on our case.

"I think the reason James Haley was murdered originated down there. The feeling of danger and corruption is palpable. He either discovered something, or was part of something, that caused people to want to kill him."

"George Adams was a Philadelphia hood. How would something that James Haley learned in Florida result in Adams coming to Paterson to kill him?"

"That's just one of a thousand questions I can't answer," I say. "But it all comes down to money. There is money all over this case, and large amounts of it."

"Drugs?" she asks.

I nod. "I can't think of anything else. But how could a sponge-diving boat, which pretty much always has tourists on board, somehow bring enough drugs into the country to generate this kind of money?"

Laurie has a good question of her own. "What was James Haley even doing in Paterson? He goes down to Florida, something happens that's so momentous that he thinks he is going to make a great deal of money, momentous enough that he becomes a target to be killed. What he does next is go to Paterson to shoot a movie about urban blight?"

"I hear you," I say. "It's not like it was so incredibly timely that it had to be done now. It's pretty fair to say that urban blight is not exactly going away. Blight seems to be the wave of the future."

"Okay, so let's assume for the moment that coming to Paterson was connected to whatever happened in Florida," she says. "That means everything he did in Paterson is part of the puzzle. That includes interviewing Joey so he could ask about drugs and Chico Simmons and also going to Christopher Tolbert's funeral."

I nod. "And we know Tolbert and Chico Simmons were connected. Zip, the gang member who led the threesome waiting to attack me outside my office, told us that Simmons was behind Tolbert's murder. So Florida is the center of the wheel, and we know there are spokes in one form or another in Philadelphia and Paterson. What we don't know is whether there are other spokes, whether those other murders that Sam found are a part of this. If they are, then this whole thing explodes."

The phone rings and Laurie looks at the Caller ID. "It's Cindy."

She hands me the phone and I say, "Hello," which is a conversation starter I have perfected over the years.

"Hello, Andy. I should not be doing this, but I feel like we owe you. I will preface this by saying that if you do not treat this confidentially, the rest of your life will be a constant misery."

"I've never felt closer to you than I do now," I say.

"Yeah. Anyway, the Bureau has opened an official investigation into the information you provided."

"Does that mean you have found connections?"

"We have confidence that those connections exist."

"And does that mean that you have found more murders, beyond the eighteen Sam discovered?"

"The total is now twenty-six, and may go higher."

"Anything else you can tell me?" I ask.

"No."

"I eagerly await further information."

"Keep awaiting," she says, and hangs up.

I hang up as well, since talking to a dead phone seems an unproductive use of my time and conversational talents.

I turn to Laurie. "The whole thing just exploded."

"Ladies and gentlemen, no one saw Joseph Gamble murder James Haley," Dylan says.

He is speaking from a podium set dead center in the courtroom, midway between the defense and prosecution tables. He only questions witnesses from there; I am much less formal, and have a tendency to pace.

"That is something on which Mr. Carpenter and I agree." Then he smiles one of his fake smiles. "That will not happen often, I assure you."

He waits for the jury to smile and silently chuckle. They are paying rapt attention now; as the testimony goes on, some of them will be fighting to stay awake. It has taken us a day and a half to choose them, seven women and five men, six African Americans, five Caucasians, and one Hispanic. It is a jury that is excellent for the prosecution or excellent for the defense, or somewhere in the middle. Anyone who thinks they can tell at this point is lying.

Dylan continues, "When a witness says something that he or she personally experiences, that is called direct evidence. Everything else is circumstantial evidence.

"In other words, to use an example that you may have heard before, if tonight before you go to bed, you look outside and see it snowing, then you will obviously know it snowed. That is direct evidence — eyewitness evidence, if you will — that it snowed.

"But let's say you go to sleep and it is not snowing and there is no snow on the ground. Then, when you wake up in the morning, there is six inches of snow on the ground. You know that it snowed during the night just as surely as if you had actually seen it snowing. That is circumstantial evidence, and it can be as reliable, even more reliable, than direct evidence.

"This is by no means unusual. When people commit crimes, they generally like to do it in secret, so that they cannot be caught and charged. It is rare that eyewitness testimony exists, and believe it or not, studies have shown that eyewitness testimony can often be wrong. People often don't see things clearly, possibly because events happen so fast or there is so much stress involved.

"The kind of evidence we will present always sees clearly and doesn't feel stress. It will prove beyond a reasonable doubt that Joseph Gamble shot and killed James Haley. Just like in my example where you knew with certainty that it snowed during the night, you will come to know with certainty that Mr. Gamble is guilty of this awful crime.

"Mr. Haley did nothing to deserve his fate. He was a hardworking man, had never been charged with or convicted of a crime in his life. Ironically, he was trying to show the world the perils and difficulties of living in an economically disadvantaged inner city, hoping to maybe contribute to making things better. That work cost him his life.

"You're going to hear some strange things in this trial. Mr. Carpenter is actually going to try to turn this into a canine caper. I kid you not." He smiles and shakes his head at the insanity of what he's just predicted I will do.

"My suggestion to you is the same suggestion you will be hearing from Judge Matthews: focus on the evidence and judge it fairly, without prejudgments or bias. You have a very serious task in front of you. As a citizen, there is nothing you can do that is more important. On behalf of Passaic

County and the State of New Jersey, I thank you for not shirking this responsibility. You are standing up and saying that the law will be followed, and that those who do not follow the law will have to face the consequences.

"I know you will do your job honorably and with dedication."

Dylan sits down, a solemn look on his face as if he has just delivered the most important message anyone will ever hear.

Judge Matthews turns to me. "Mr. Carpenter, do you wish to give your opening statement now?"

"Yes, thank you, Your Honor."

I always take this option, rather than waiting until the beginning of the defense case, because I don't want the prosecution's opening statement to stand unrefuted. It's bad enough that they will be parading a long series of witnesses and evidence against Joey; I need the jury to know there is another side to the story.

In this situation, it's even more important that I speak now. Judges guard their calendar days like they are gold bullion. It's Friday today, and I was hoping that Judge Matthews would delay the opening arguments until Monday. But the idea of today being wasted was abhorrent to her.

Because of that, the jury is going to have this weekend with nothing to consider other than the opening statements. I can't have them pondering only the prosecution's point of view and not ours too; they need to spend the next two days knowing that this trial is not going to be a walkover, but rather a pitched battle.

I also think that Joey's grandmother Cynthia Gamble, sitting directly behind the defense table, will leap to her feet and strangle me if I don't immediately start to say good things about her grandson. And as far as I know, Marcus is not here to protect me.

"Ladies and gentlemen, I'd like to start by picking up where Mr. Campbell left off in his discussion of circumstantial evidence. And I may surprise you by not saying that it's never accurate or significant. It is a fallacy that eyewitness evidence is always preferable.

"But on the other hand, all evidence should be viewed with skepticism. Your job is to analyze it, to judge its merits, not just to take it at face value. That's why you are here, and that's why, when you came to court today, you brought your brain and your logic and your common sense with you.

"Let's take Mr. Campbell's hypothetical about snow during the night. Let's put a little twist on it. You're an actor or actress; let's say you're filming a sequel to *White Christmas.* You leave the set in the evening and there's no snow on the ground, but when you come back in the morning, the ground is covered with snow, so you know it snowed during the night.

"But then you find out that the group of professional set decorators working on the movie brought the snow in during the night because it was needed for the next scene. I mean, after all, you're filming *White Christmas.*

"So the professionals made it appear that it had snowed, even though it hadn't. That means that in this instance, Mr. Campbell's circumstantial evidence would have led you in the wrong direction.

"We all understand that this is not a movie set and everything is real, but the principle remains the same. The evidence may seem to be there, may even seem to be compelling, but you have to look deeper, using your brain and your logic and your common sense.

"The evidence against Joey Gamble is circumstantial. Mr. Campbell admitted that, and I commend him for doing so. But how did it come about? Were there people who created it, like the professionals on the movie set? Yes, there were, and you will hear about them. Better yet, not only will we offer you ample cause to have reasonable doubt about Joey Gamble's guilt, we will even tell you who actually committed the crime.

"I would not be telling you all of this if I didn't believe that I could deliver it, so at the end of the trial, I will recount in my closing statement exactly how I did that.

"But for now, the focus is on Joey Gamble, even though he has done nothing to deserve this. He has never in his life been convicted of a crime. No one has ever accused him of committing any act of violence. He has lived his entire life in a neighborhood rife with gangs and crime, and has resisted all of it. He is working to earn money for college, which is his dream.

"But events made him a convenient target, someone to blame for the terrible act of murdering James Haley. And the police and Mr. Campbell fell for it, because that's what was intended by the professional criminals who planted the evidence that Mr. Campbell will put before you. You will hear both sides, and I am confident that you will have more than a reasonable doubt as to Mr.

Gamble's guilt.

"Thank you for listening."

290

Jack Hagans, the investigator I hired in Florida, calls in with his first report.

Since Laurie is in charge of the investigations end, I want him to deal with her, so I introduce them on the phone. She has independently checked him out since I got back and has gotten nothing but good feedback.

Since I am familiar with the setup down in Florida and Laurie isn't, I stay on the line. Hopefully I won't have to do this in the future.

"I'll send you my report electronically and in full detail," Hagans says, "but at this point I would describe the operation as uneventful, with one notable exception, which I'll get to. I've begun surveillance on the *Ginny May* each morning at seven A.M., though the crewmen don't start to arrive until close to nine. Moving forward I can start later, if you want me to.

"The boat has gone out each day at eleven, as advertised, with anywhere from six to ten tourists on board, along with three crewmen. Obviously I can't maintain the surveillance while they're at sea, but their literature says that they are doing commercial sponge diving while teaching the observers the process. Those tourists, or observers, do not get to do any actual diving. The boat returns each day at four with the tourists and the sponge haul for the day."

I'm sure I will have questions, but at this point I don't interrupt. Hagans sounds very competent and is giving us the information clearly and concisely, the way I like it.

"As the crew disperses, I obviously can't follow all of them, so I have alternated. They are predictable; one of them goes to a bar about a block away from where the boat is docked, while the other two take the sponges they've collected to a warehouse set off from the road on the way to Tarpon Springs. They store them there and then head back to the bar to join their friend.

"They stay at the bar until around ten o'clock, then leave and go their own separate ways. One of them always drives to that same warehouse, pulls up outside, but does not go in. There are light sensors on the building, so his car sets them off.

"Yesterday, while the boat was out, I went to the warehouse to see if I could determine anything unusual about it. I was able to make some observations from a distance, through a window, using high-powered binoculars. I found nothing out of the ordinary; there are cartons of what appear to be sponges stored there. I did not attempt to enter.

"There is an alarm system that could be circumvented, but there are some risks of discovery attached to that, so I didn't want to do so without your requesting it. There are also video cameras set up outside and I would think very likely inside as well."

"Can you send us a photograph of the warehouse and an address?" Laurie asks.

"It will be in the electronic report."

"You said earlier that your report was uneventful, with one notable exception," I say. "What were you referring to?"

"The media reported this morning that a body turned up on shore during the night, brought in by the tide. The police are not at this point revealing details, but I am told that foul play is suspected."

I'm not about to tell him that this is the work of Marcus, and that the body is that of the man who tried to kill Lorna Diaz.

"Has he been identified?"

"Yes. He was the fourth member of the *Ginny May* crew." He pauses, and then adds rather pointedly, "Is there anything I should know about this?"

"Anything you can find out about it would be very helpful," Laurie says, noncommittally.

"Understood. I'll check with my sources down here."

Laurie thanks Hagans and compliments him on his work. She asks him to keep doing what he's doing and to report to us both electronically and by phone.

We get off the phone and I ask Laurie what she thinks. "I think he's professional and doing the job he's supposed to be doing. And I don't think we know any more than we did before he called. Other than that a body has been found."

I nod. "Boy, that puts things into perspective, doesn't it? One minute you're trying to strangle a woman in an alley, and the next thing you know, your body is washing up on shore."

"Marcus would not have done it if it wasn't necessary," Laurie says. I know she believes that, but she also is re-convincing herself of it. As an ex-cop, Laurie is just naturally uncomfortable with a killing of any type, for any reason, not being adjudicated by the justice system.

"The guy would have killed Lorna Diaz," I say. "There is no doubt about it." Then, "But we need to talk about Marcus."

"What about him?"

"I know he's watching me, and I get that I need some watching, but we need to make better use of his time."

"How so?" she asks, with obvious suspicion.

"I'm going to be in court all day; I don't need protection then. And when I'm home, where you and your gun reside, I'm pretty safe as well. Plus, as you know, I can handle myself pretty well."

"You just blew your argument."

I nod. "Yeah, I tried to slip that last one in. But I would rather that Marcus was tailing Chico Simmons."

"Why?"

"Because we've started the trial and we are basically nowhere. We know that James Haley learned something that got him killed, and we know he was interested in Chico Simmons and Christopher Tolbert. And we know that Chico had Tolbert killed. So I admit I am throwing things against the wall and hoping something sticks, but Chico is involved in this and maybe Marcus will catch him making a mistake, and . . ."

"And?"

"And I don't have a better idea."

She nods. "Neither do I. I'll talk to Marcus."

"We call Mr. Darryl Holland," Dylan says.

Holland is going to be an uncontroversial witness, and the fact that Dylan is calling him is logical and straight out of the prosecutorial textbook. He is going to build his case from the beginning.

Dylan shows a map of the neighborhood and gets Holland to identify where he lives and where James Haley had been living at the time of his death. The houses were almost directly around the block from each other. There is a fairly large common area behind all of the houses, which is to say in the center of the square block.

Dylan brings him to the night in question. "So that night you were walking in this area, between all the houses?"

"Yes."

"Why?"

"I was walking my dog. Many of the neighbors walked their dogs there; it was fairly common. I did it every night."

Dylan nods. "What did you see when you passed Mr. Haley's back door?"

"Well, at first I saw that it was open, so I was half expecting him to come out. It's usually closed, so I thought maybe he had just opened it. He could have forgotten something and gone back in to get it."

"Did he come out?"

"No, so I walked over. There was a chance that he didn't realize it was open, so I was going to call in to him."

"You knew Mr. Haley?"

"I wouldn't say I knew him; he had only been living there a very short time. But I had seen him and said hello a couple of times."

"It was dark that night in the back?"

"Yes. It was a cloudy night, so very little moonlight. There was some light coming from the houses, but not much."

"Was there a light in the doorway of Mr. Haley's house?" Dylan asked.

"Yes. It was bright. When I went to it, it took me a few moments to adjust my eyes to the light when I looked inside."

"What did you see?"

"Inside the back hallway, about fifteen or so feet from the door, I saw Mr. Haley. I didn't know it was him, of course, because he was facedown. There was blood coming from him onto the floor; it looked like it might be coming from his head, but I couldn't be sure."

"What did you do?"

"Well, at first I didn't know what to do, whether to go to him or run home and call nine-one-one. I didn't have my cell phone with me," Holland says. "I'm afraid I panicked. But I don't know first aid, so it seemed like the way I could be most helpful was to call nine-one-one."

"Did you do that?"

"I did. I ran home and called, and then went back to the house to direct the police to Mr. Haley's back door. They were there just a couple of minutes after I got back."

Holland has nothing more to offer. Once the police came, they heard what he had to say and then kept him out of the way. Every other neighbor in the area soon came down and joined him, though they were all prevented from getting close enough to see anything.

Dylan turns him over to me. There's nothing there for me to attack, or any reason to try to discredit him, but I do have a point to make.

"Mr. Holland, did you see anyone in or

around Mr. Haley's house besides Mr. Haley?"

He shakes his head. "I did not."

"How long were you out in this back area before you saw the open door?"

"I had just gotten out there, so maybe two minutes?"

"And the door was already open? You didn't see it open while you were out there?"

"It was already open."

"So it could have been open five or ten minutes before you saw it? You'd have no way of knowing?"

"Correct," he says.

"So someone else, presumably the person who shot Mr. Haley, could have left through the back door, just as they came in, without you seeing that person?"

Dylan objects that we have no way of knowing whether the killer came in through the back door, that there is no testimony to that effect. It is a silly objection, since he himself is going to introduce evidence later showing the door was broken into.

I smile my most condescending smile, and throw in a condescending slight head shake. It's a difficult maneuver, which I learned in law school when I took Condescending Smile and Head Shake 101. Then I rephrase the question and Holland agrees that someone could have left without him seeing the person.

"You said you had conversed with Mr. Haley on a couple of occasions. How did you come to do that?"

"We were both walking our dogs."

"Mr. Haley had a dog?"

"Yes. A French bulldog. He and my dog got along really well."

"Do you know his dog's name?"

He nods. "Truman."

"Did you see Truman that night? Was he in the back hallway?"

"No."

"Did you hear him barking?"

"No."

"Thank you. No further questions."

I've gotten in front of the jury that Haley had a dog, that the dog's name was Truman, and that he wasn't around after the murder.

Just call me Clarence Darrow.

We have no standing to get discovery information on the Christopher Tolbert murder.

I just cannot announce a connection between the homeless man whose body turned up in Nash Park in Clifton to the James Haley murder in Paterson.

The fact that Haley went to Tolbert's funeral would clearly not be compelling enough to the court, and I can't use the fact that Zip connected Chico Simmons to Tolbert's death, nor can I use the apparent rash of similar killings around the country.

That is why I am in the office of the Passaic County coroner, Janet Carlson. Janet is a friend, and without a doubt the best-looking coroner in the history of Earth. I know it's sexist to say this, but if there was a "Miss Coroner" contest, she would have retired the trophy years ago.

She is also extremely competent and an excellent witness. She will be testifying for the prosecution in our trial, and I am just glad that I won't need to challenge her testimony, because as expert witnesses go, she is rock solid.

I made the appointment through her assistant, and though Janet greets me warmly, she says, "You know I can't talk about my testimony with you, Andy. Dylan would have a stroke."

"We certainly don't want to do anything to harm Dylan," I say. "But I'm actually here to talk about the Tolbert killing."

She thinks for a moment and then nods. "Nash Park? Why are you involved in that?"

"You know me. I just love murders of all kinds."

She laughs. "What do you want to know?"

"Anything you can tell me." The truth is that the autopsy results are not sealed; they are open to the public. All I'm asking for is an advance preview.

She asks for the file to be sent to her. She didn't do the autopsy herself; it was done by one of her assistants. Once she gets the file, she looks through it slowly and carefully. Janet does not talk about her work lightly or casually; whether on the stand or sitting in her office, she likes to be accurate.

"Gunshot wound to the head was the cause of death, Andy. No bruises, scrapes, or signs of a fight. Death was about four hours before discovery and did not likely take place where the body was discovered."

"Did you run toxicology?"

She looks at me with annoyance. "Of course."

"Drugs?"

She looks at the report, probably for the first time. "No, all clean." Then, after a few more moments of reading, "That's strange."

"What is?" I ask, though I suspect she will tell me anyway.

"There are traces of amephrotane; it's a natural compound that is a component of a number of opioids."

"So it's likely Tolbert was taking opioids?

She shakes her head. "No. If he was, there would be other chemicals present. There's no reason the amephrotane would outlast the others, so to speak."

"Is there any other way to ingest amephrotane?" I ask.

"Yes," she said. "It's prevalent in certain types of green vegetables."

"Laurie must be loaded with the stuff. She's one of those weirdos who cares about what they put into their bodies and think good health is important."

Janet doesn't respond; she's ignoring me even though I think I'm doing some damn good bantering. Instead she just keeps reading the report in front of her.

So I give it another shot. "And then those people — I call them health-ites — it's not enough that they're healthy. They want everybody else to be healthy also. Talk about selfish."

Not a word out of her. I should be writing this stuff down to use in future bantering sessions with more receptive audiences. Possibly when the person I'm bantering with is not reading about a grisly death.

"I'm going to have to talk to Charles about this," she finally says.

"Who is Charles?"

"He did the autopsy; there's an unusual aspect of it that I want to discuss with him, since he saw it firsthand."

"What is it?"

"There are indications of emesis, internal and external. It was even on his clothing. Then there are signs of intense perspiration, enlarged tear ducts."

"Emesis?"

"Vomiting," she says.

"Signs of stress?" I ask. "Maybe because he knew he was going to be killed?"

She nods. "It's possible. But it feels more like drug or alcohol withdrawal, yet the toxicology says otherwise. Very strange."

She promises to keep me posted if Charles has any further insight into the situation. Before I leave, I make her write out the word *amephrotane.*

I head down to the office to pick up some more discovery documents that have come in, but on the way I call Laurie. I tell her about my meeting with Janet and ask if she will call Sergeant Rubin in Philadelphia.

"Please ask him to check the toxicology reports on the homeless murder victims. I want to know if there were any drugs present, and I especially want to know if there is any trace of amephrotane."

"Can you spell it?" she asks.

"Of course I can spell it."

Dylan's next witness is Officer Patricia Jonas.

Jonas has only been on the force for three years and likely has rarely testified in this kind of consequential case, but this is going to be an easy way for her to gain experience. She and her partner were the first officers on the scene, responding to Darryl Holland's 911 call.

She testifies to that effect, describing how they arrived on the scene, talked to Holland, and then quickly assessed the situation.

"Mr. Haley was deceased when you arrived, is that correct?"

"Without question. I reported in to Homicide and then called for an ambulance and the coroner, knowing it was the coroner that would unfortunately be needed."

"What did you do once you determined that Mr. Haley was deceased?"

"We checked the rest of the house to confirm that the perpetrator was not still on the scene. Then we cordoned off the area and made sure that the neighbors, who had started to gather, were set back."

"The perpetrator was gone?"

She nods. "Yes."

"Did you notice anything else unusual about the house as you looked through it?" Dylan asks.

"It certainly appeared to have been ransacked."

"It looked like a robbery scene?" Dylan asks.

"Absolutely."

"Could you determine if anything was missing?"

She shakes her head. "That was not our role. We were simply there to secure the scene for the detectives."

My turn. "Officer Jonas, you said that the house looked as if it had been ransacked and that it seemed to be a robbery scene. Is that correct?"

"Yes."

"What does a ransacked robbery scene look like?"

"Things thrown around, drawers opened and dumped on the floor, things like that," she says.

"So if I went home tonight and opened drawers, dumped things on the floor, that kind of thing, it might look like I had been robbed?"

"Possibly."

"Even if I hadn't been robbed?"

"I suppose so."

"The area where you found Mr. Haley's body . . . was that a living area in the house?"

"I'm not sure what you mean."

"Sorry, I wasn't clear. Was there a television there? A couch? A table? Was that an area where a person might hang out?"

She shakes her head. "No, it is basically a hallway."

"So it seems likely that he went down there because someone was coming in through the back door?"

"I can't know for sure."

"Can you think of another reason he might have been there?"

"No. Not at the moment."

"There has been testimony that Mr. Haley owned a dog. Are you aware of that?"

"I didn't hear the testimony," she says, "but I saw a dog's water dish in the house."

"Did you see the dog while you were there?"

"No."

"Did you look for him?"

"No. I assumed he was either not there, or hiding. But I had other things I needed to do."

"Thank you."

Dylan calls Officer Jonas's partner to the stand, for no other purpose than to basically repeat everything she just said. It doesn't do us any additional damage, and even though I am able to once again get across the fact that Truman was nowhere to be found, it doesn't help us much either.

Dylan's next witness is actually a bit of a surprise, though he was obviously on the witness list. It's another neighbor of Haley's, a longtime resident of the area named Jeff Traynor.

He establishes that Traynor was also walking his dog that night; does no one in that neighborhood have cats? But Traynor was out front and claims to have seen Joey Gamble leave the house through the front door.

"Wasn't it dark that night?" Dylan asks.

"I suppose it was, but there is a streetlight very close to that house, and there was a porch light on as well. I had no trouble seeing."

"And you're sure it was Mr. Gamble?"

"Positive. We even made eye contact; I got

a very good look at him."

If I were Dylan, I would not have called Traynor to the stand. He doesn't need him to establish Joey's presence at the scene; he has fingerprint evidence to that effect. I think it's overkill, and it establishes an opening for me.

I could attack it by questioning whether Traynor can be sure of the identification; he saw him briefly, at night, etc. But then I'd be making the same mistake as Dylan. I'm going to admit Joey was there, so why try to cast doubt on a witness who saw him there?

I start my questions off easy. "Mr. Traynor, was Mr. Gamble running when you saw him leave the house?"

"No."

"Did he seem to be in a hurry?"

"Not that I could tell."

"Did you see where he went after he left? Did he go to a car?"

"I didn't notice; I was heading back to my own house."

"But he definitely left through the front door?"

"Definitely."

"You said that you made eye contact with him? So you believe he knew that you saw him?"

"I certainly think so. We were within

twenty feet of each other, and like I said, we looked right at each other."

"He made no effort to conceal his identity?" I ask. "Cover his face? Anything like that?"

"No."

"And even though he knew that you saw him close up and could therefore identify him, he didn't try to attack you?"

"Definitely not."

"Did he have a dog with him?" I ask.

"No. I didn't see a dog."

"Thank you."

Dylan did very little to hurt us today, but these are still just the prelims. There are other, more substantive witnesses coming later who are going to damage us badly, if not fatally. For the time being, all we will be able to do is play defense. But that won't be enough, not by a long shot.

If we're going to win this thing, we are going to have to win on offense, by making an affirmative case that can sway the jury.

Once I'm out of the courtroom, I check my cell phone and there's a message from Laurie, asking me to call.

"Rubin got back to me," she says. "No drugs found in either of the two victims, but there were traces of amephrotane. He asked me what it meant. I didn't know what

to tell him, because I don't have the slightest idea."

"I don't either, not yet. But I can spell it."

In addition to Janet's analysis of the autopsy results and the present of amephrotane, we're coming up with some interesting information regarding the murder of Christopher Tolbert.

Laurie talked to the director of the homeless shelter where Tolbert often took his meals. No one had seen Tolbert for at least six days before his body was discovered.

I ask Laurie to call Cindy Spodek to ask her if the autopsy results for the other homicides in other cities also show the presence of amephrotane.

Of course, my delight at making progress on Tolbert's murder is tempered somewhat by the fact that our client is on trial for the James Haley murder. The connection between our case and Tolbert has been tenuous from the beginning and remains so; at this point our chance of getting evidence about Tolbert admitted in our trial remains zero.

Today is the last day that Dylan will be setting up his case before he calls in the big guns. Janet Carlson is his first witness, and she is here to say that the body with gunshot wounds in the back and head died from gunshot wounds to the back and head.

Actually, that is not Dylan's reason for having her here at all. He has chosen to use Janet's appearance to introduce the crime scene photos. Of course, on an evidentiary level it's unnecessary; the jury knows what happened to Haley and does not need to see photos of it.

But it is a time-honored prosecutorial maneuver. Seeing the gory scene is designed to make the jury revolted and angry, and the only person available to them to take their anger out on is the defendant — in this case, Joey Gamble.

I have no questions for Janet; what she said was self-evident and my not bothering to question her hopefully says to the jury that it is unimportant to the overall case. The jury knew Haley was murdered before she testified and they knew it after she testified. She did not in any way incriminate Joey.

Next up is Joey's sometime friend Archie

Sandler. Sandler is dressed in a suit and tie, which is way too tight on him; I wouldn't be surprised if it were one of Dylan's. Sandler looks like he'd rather be anywhere else in the world than in this courtroom.

Dylan gets Sandler to say that Joey told him he was going to see James Haley that night. According to Sandler, Joey didn't tell him why he was going. "Were people annoyed that Mr. Haley was in the neighborhood?"

Sandler nods. "I guess so. Some guys were talking."

Dylan asks, "Was Mr. Gamble one of the people who was talking?"

"I don't remember."

"You and Mr. Gamble are good friends?" Dylan asks.

"Yeah, I guess. We're cool."

My first question for Sandler is, "Did Mr. Gamble tell you he was going to steal from Mr. Haley?"

"No."

"Did he say he was going to hurt Mr. Haley?"

"No."

"Did he say he was going to kill Mr. Haley?"

"No."

"Did he tell you not to tell anyone he was

316

going to Mr. Haley's that night?"

"No."

"Did you see Mr. Gamble at the bar later that night?"

"Yeah, he was there."

"Did he act unusual in any way? Did he confide in you that something had happened?"

"No."

I let Sandler off the stand and the judge sends us out to a late lunch. There will be a couple of additional witnesses afterward, one of whom will reconfirm Sandler's testimony that Joey spoke to Haley on the Paterson streets the day of the murder. The other witness will simply say that Joey was expected to join his friends at a local bar that night, as he often did, but that he got there after the time of death that the coroner established.

Tomorrow will be the detective in charge of the case and the forensic evidence. Or, as Dylan and everyone else would view it, the big guns.

Mateo Rojas knew that including Paterson was a mistake in the first place.

For one thing, its size alone should have disqualified it. It is a decent-sized city, the 174th largest in the US by population, but that should have been barely enough to get it into the third or fourth wave.

The city also did not provide anyone who possessed the structure and maturity that the operation demanded. Chico Simmons commanded a loose and unfocused operation, held together by fear of his ruthlessness. Now he was being called on to run an enterprise that also required business competence, and he was simply not up to the task.

Frank Silvio had wanted to include Paterson, and Rojas had gone along. Silvio was Rojas's biggest mistake, and biggest surprise. There were five men under Rojas on that level, Silvio and four others. Rojas had handpicked all of them, and when this began, he would have said that Silvio was the best of the bunch.

He was wrong.

Silvio had made mistakes. Choosing Paterson and Chico was one of them, and George Adams was another. Those mistakes led to others and eventually had led to a situation that was unacceptable. A lawyer and his investigators were digging into the case, investigating Silvio and Chico and others. A trial was being conducted, which could only bring publicity and more unwanted attention.

The operation was now in the end game, so Rojas had to adjust his risk assessments accordingly. The threat was now more in the post-operation phase; the danger was the possible discovery of those responsible by law enforcement.

In other words, Rojas and his people were vulnerable.

That was why Rojas had called this meeting between himself, Silvio, and Chico Simmons. They were to come with their suggestions for a way forward and were informed that final decisions would be made and then implementation would proceed. They were instructed to come alone, and not to share the outcome of the discussion with anyone.

The meeting was held in a four-store strip mall in Lyndhurst that was notable for the fact that all four stores were empty and available for lease. Rojas had scouted it out and deemed it perfect, since it was off the beaten path with little street traffic. The small parking lot out front was occasionally used by people looking to avoid the cost of metered street parking, so some minor activity would go relatively unnoticed.

Rojas had no difficulty getting through the lock on the store farthest to the left, which had most recently been a pet store. Then he waited for Silvio and Simmons, who had been instructed to arrive twenty minutes apart, with Silvio arriving first.

Silvio appeared on time and was dead before he stepped three feet into the store. Rojas had considered questioning him first, since he had some information that would have been helpful. But Rojas respected the fact that Silvio was a dangerous man; it was a major reason he had hired him in the first place. Best to kill him before he had a chance to get his bearings, or to realize the danger he was in.

Rojas used a silencer on his handgun so as not to attract attention. He then moved Silvio's body so that it would not be within

Simmons's sight line when he showed up. Bloodstains remained on the floor, but Rojas was not concerned that Simmons would make the connection and understand the danger in the few seconds he would have to live.

Simmons did not do exactly as instructed. He was not as confident in his ability to protect himself, nor was he completely trusting of Rojas. So even though he had been told to come alone, he brought one of his lieutenants with him.

That brought the number of people Rojas killed in that room to three.

Rojas made no effort to conceal the bodies. Once he was a distance from the store, he was going to call 911 and anonymously report that the murders had taken place in that location. He wanted to be sure that Gamble's lawyer knew they were dead; it would leave them no one to look for, and no one to investigate. Silvio and Simmons had come to represent weak links, so Rojas had removed them from the chain.

The lawyer would not be looking for Rojas because he did not know Rojas existed.

So Rojas left to call 911, and as he did, he had no idea that Marcus Clark was taking his picture.

The triple murder was obviously a field day for the media.

Cold-blooded assassinations like this do not happen every day, so that in itself would have made it the lead story on every newscast. But the identities of two of the victims elevated it to a monster story. One was a local gang leader, and another was an organized crime figure known for his ruthlessness.

The latter, Frank Silvio, had one other thing about him that made him fairly unique among murder victims. He was known to already have been dead for six months.

Laurie and I didn't have to wait for the media reports to know what happened. Marcus had come over to report his version of events. He had followed Chico Simmons to the strip mall. He watched him and another guy go in and then, within a few minutes, saw someone else come out.

Marcus, being Marcus, was smart enough to get a picture of the guy who left.

He did not follow him because he had no way of knowing that Simmons or anyone else had been murdered in the store. The killer had apparently used a silencer. Marcus also obviously had no way to know that Frank Silvio was one of the victims, because he had followed Chico to the scene, and Silvio must have gotten there earlier.

Within minutes, police cars were everywhere, so Marcus assumed that the killer himself had called 911. Apparently the killer wanted everyone to know that Silvio and Simmons had departed this earth.

After Marcus leaves, Laurie and I sit down to discuss the situation. "For the moment, at least, it's an overall negative," I say. "We can't connect Silvio or Simmons to our case based on enough evidence to make it admissible, so it's a nonfactor in the trial. Jurors could even read these reports without realizing it has anything to do with the trial they're sitting on. So the publicity about it does not help us."

"So how do you see it as a negative?" she asks.

"It cuts off our avenues of investigation. We knew about Silvio and Simmons, so we could be looking for them, hoping they'd make a mistake to give us an opening. That's why we had Marcus following Simmons. But now it's safe to say that they are done making mistakes."

"I don't understand why this guy would kill them."

"Maybe to announce to the world that they were dead, so that no one, including us, would be looking for them anymore. And more important, they were obviously no longer necessary, which has to mean that whatever they're doing has moved into a new phase."

In terms of the photograph itself, Laurie thinks we have an obligation to give it to the police; it is evidence in a murder case. I agree, but disagree on the timing. That photograph may be something we can use later on as part of a trade. Eventually we will do the right thing and give up the photograph, but right now we have to recognize that our first obligation is to our client.

Laurie goes along with me, at least for the moment. Ricky calls out to me from his bedroom; I wasn't home when he went to bed, so I missed our tuck-in routine. Usually we talk for at least ten minutes before he goes to sleep. Very often my conversation actually puts him to sleep.

He's woken up and wants to have our talk, albeit a little late. He asks me what I did today, and since it involves multiple murders, I deflect by saying I had to be in court a lot, and boy, was it boring.

He tells me that he spent an hour after school at Will Rubenstein's house, playing some new video game. "It's great, Dad. Can I get it when it comes out?"

"If it's not out yet, how does Will have it already?"

"He won it in some contest. He's lucky," Ricky says.

I'm sure that's the plan of the diabolical game makers. They come up with ways to get a few thousand copies out there in advance so that millions of kids can hear about it and beg their parents for it.

I tell him he has to ask his mother if he can have the game. She checks out how violent they are and limits the time he can play, so it's not an area I like to involve myself in. I don't tell him that he has just triggered something in my mind.

I hear the phone ringing, but Laurie picks it up after one ring. I say good night to Ricky, give him a kiss on the forehead, and tell him I love him. It's a ritual I'm hoping to be able to continue until he's in his mid-fifties.

I leave his room and gather the leashes to take Tara and Sebastian for their evening walk. That is delayed when Laurie comes to me with the phone and says, "It's Cindy Spodek. It's about the amephrotane."

We had asked Cindy if the blood tests on any of the other murdered homeless men had shown the presence of amephrotane, as it did in Tolbert's and the Philadelphia cases.

When I get on the phone, Cindy says, "Andy, you seem to have struck a nerve by asking about the amephrotane. It showed up in almost all of the other cases."

"I'm not surprised."

"DEA got word of it and they're very interested. They want to talk to you," she says.

"What about?"

"They think you might be able to help them. I don't know any more than that."

"Can you give them a message for me? Tell them I said tough shit."

Laurie is standing near me, listening to my end of the conversation. She does a double take when she hears what I said.

"Excuse me?"

"Sorry, Laurie always tells me I mumble a lot. What I said was, 'Tell them I said tough shit.' "

"You won't meet with them?"

"What tipped you off?"

"Is there a problem here?" she asks, obviously annoyed with me.

"Yes, there's a problem. Remember when all this started and we talked about a quid pro quo? Well, I've done plenty of quidding, but your side hasn't done any pro-quo-ing. And meanwhile my client is twisting in the wind."

"Andy, I think you're making a mistake here."

"You know what, maybe you're right. Maybe I shouldn't just refuse; maybe I should put conditions on this. So here's my condition: You, or they, get me the following information for every single murder of a homeless person that fits the pattern. I want copies of the autopsy and toxicology reports, whether they had been thought by friends or family to have been drug addicts, and when they were last reported as having been seen alive. They get me all that, or you get me all that, and I'll meet with them. And they will be happy with what I have to tell them, believe me."

"Andy, these are not people you can dictate terms to, and I am not either."

"Sorry, Cindy, but this is the way it's going to be. If they don't want me to dictate the terms of our meeting, then they don't have to meet with me. We can all go our separate ways. Oh, and Laurie is going to scan and send you a photograph of a guy. When they want to talk to me about him, if they haven't met my conditions, you can refer them to my previous comment about 'tough shit.' "

I hang up and hand the phone to Laurie. "What the hell was that?" she asks.

"Wrong number."

"You said they're going to be happy with what you have to tell them? Why exactly is that?"

"Because Ricky just solved the whole case for me. Oh, and we need Marcus to go back down to Florida. And he should take Willie with him."

I call Willie and explain the situation. He's all too happy to go to Florida with Marcus. Willie loves getting in on the action almost as much as Sam does, the difference being that Willie can handle himself. Willie even likes hanging around with Marcus.

Laurie makes the call to Marcus, and we book the flights.

And for the first time in a while, I'm feeling pretty damn good about things. Of course, it won't last. It never does.

Sergeant Xavier Jennings has been working in forensics on the Paterson police force forever.

I think he was already here when Urban Blight, idiot son of Nehemiah and Rebecca Blight, discovered the place. Jennings is approaching retirement age and it's likely that every defense attorney in the county, including me, will chip in and throw him a party. Just the fact that we would never have to see him on a witness stand again would be cause for celebration.

Jennings is competent and unflappable, two annoying traits in a police witness. If you're scoring at home, put me down as preferring incompetent and ultraflappable.

Dylan is going to use Jennings to place Joey at the murder scene, and it will be a piece of cake for Jennings to do so. Dylan takes him through his fingerprint identification work and asks if Joey's prints were at the scene.

"Yes," Jennings says. "In fourteen locations in the house."

"Did you match the prints before Mr. Gamble was arrested?"

"Yes. His prints were in the system from some previous charges."

I could object to this; it is a cheap and unethical way for Dylan to get "prior bad acts" in, when they would have been inadmissible if introduced by other means. But I'll deal with it in cross-examination.

"Did you find Mr. Gamble's DNA in the house as well?"

"We did."

"Is there any doubt in your mind that Mr. Gamble was in the victim's house?"

"None whatsoever."

"Thank you."

I start my cross with, "Sergeant Jennings, how many different sets of fingerprints did you find in that house?"

"Well, the house was rented out a lot, so . . ."

"Sergeant Jennings, if Mr. Campbell or I want to know the history of the house, we can call a real estate agent to the stand. You're here to answer questions about your work, so let's start over. How many different sets of fingerprints did you find in that house?"

"Seventeen."

"Seventeen different people?"

"Yes."

"Did some of them leave prints in multiple locations in the house?"

"Yes."

"Based on your work, were any of those seventeen other people in the house that night?" I ask.

"I couldn't say."

"Based on your work, was Mr. Gamble in the house that night?"

"I couldn't say."

I nod. "Because you don't know when all those prints were left, is that correct?"

"Yes."

"As I'm sure you know, Mr. Haley's body was found in the hallway near the back door," I say. "Were Mr. Gamble's prints found back there?"

"No."

"The back door lock was broken. Were Mr. Gamble's prints found on the door?"

"No."

"So if he was in either of those places, he took care to make sure he did not leave prints?"

"I couldn't say."

"How long have you been doing forensics for the Paterson police, Sergeant Jennings?"

"Thirty-six years."

"Based on all those years of experience, can you think of a reason why a person would take care not to leave prints in the back hallway and on the back door, yet would happily leave them everywhere else in the house?"

He surprises me by smiling the smile of somebody near retirement age who doesn't really give a shit. "I just lift the prints," he says. "I don't explain them."

I return the smile. "By the way, Sergeant, you testified that Mr. Gamble's prints were on file. It was a way for Mr. Campbell to get the jury to incorrectly believe that he had a criminal record. Do you remember that?"

Dylan jumps out of his seat, objecting and acting wounded by the accusation. The judge sustains the objection, and I rephrase.

"Do you remember your testimony in that regard?"

"Yes."

"Are you aware that while Mr. Gamble was interrogated by police in the past, he was never actually charged with a crime?"

Dylan objects again, this time stating that the question assumes facts not in evidence.

The objection is sustained, so I again re-phrase.

"Sergeant, to your knowledge, has Mr. Gamble ever been charged with a crime before this?"

"No, he has not."

"Thank you," I say, as I stare at Dylan in silent reproach. My silent reproach stares are not as good as Laurie's, but I'm learning from the master.

I let Jennings off the stand. I did some damage, which I'm pleased with, but I'm sure Dylan is pleased as well. He placed Joey in the house, which means Joey was physically in a position to have committed the crime.

My difficulty is going to be getting the actual reason for Joey's being there — his being interviewed by Haley — in front of the jury without putting Joey on the stand.

But first I have to get through this afternoon.

Lieutenant Luther Crenshaw has been described by Pete Stanton as the best cop in his department.

Pete was including himself in that assessment, and Pete thinks rather highly of himself. Crenshaw is that good.

Unfortunately, he was also the detective assigned to supervise the James Haley murder investigation, and he's in court to tell the jury what went into it and why they should put Joey Gamble in jail for the rest of his life.

"Lieutenant Crenshaw, did you execute a search warrant on the house of Joseph Gamble?"

"Yes, pursuant to a court order. We were investigating the homicide of James Haley two nights earlier."

"You suspected Mr. Gamble of having committed the homicide?"

"Yes, based on fingerprint evidence at the

scene and a witness report identifying Mr. Gamble as having left Mr. Haley's house at around the time of the shooting."

Dylan takes four more questions to get Crenshaw to say what he could have gotten in just one: that he found possessions belonging to Haley, including his wallet, and a .38-caliber revolver buried behind Gamble's garage. He also says that ballistics tests demonstrated that the same weapon fired the fatal bullets into Mr. Haley.

Then Dylan reverses the chronology and has Crenshaw describe the murder scene, including his theory of how the murder took place. It's not surprising; he believes Joey broke in through the back door, was met by Haley, and gunned him down in the back hallway.

"It's possible he did not realize that Mr. Haley was at home; there's no way for us to know that. But once he was discovered and shot the victim, he then went upstairs and ransacked the place, taking certain items with him."

"So you believe it was a robbery gone bad?" Dylan asks.

"I believe it was an armed robbery gone bad. But in my experience, a thief does not bring a loaded weapon to commit a burglary unless he is willing to use it. In this case, the perpetrator was willing to use it."

"Lieutenant Crenshaw," I say after Dylan turns the witness over to me, "let's talk some more about your theory of the events in question. You've testified that the killer came in the back door by breaking the lock, was surprised by Mr. Haley, and shot him right there. Correct?"

"Yes."

"And there was a light on in the hall?" I ask.

"Yes."

"What is your theory as to why the killer left the back door open when he went into the house to burglarize it?"

"Hard to say. Maybe he was panicked at having just killed Mr. Haley and didn't realize that he hadn't closed it."

"But not panicked enough to just leave and not follow through on the robbery?"

"The robbery was why he was there," Crenshaw says.

"Or perhaps he wanted to make the robbery *look* like the reason he was there," I say. Dylan objects that I am testifying for the witness, and Judge Matthews sustains the objection.

"Is it possible that the killer did not, in fact, leave the door open at that point, but instead left it open later on, when he left the house?"

"He left through the front. A witness testified to that."

"No, the witness testified that Mr. Gamble left through the front. He didn't say anything about the killer; at that point, he wasn't even aware there had been a killing. But I'm sorry, I didn't mean to suggest something that doesn't fit your preconceived theories of the case."

Another sustained objection from Dylan; business as usual.

I move on. "Lieutenant, Mr. Haley had a very expensive video camera that was not taken. Any theories on that?"

He shrugs. "Might have been too large, and could have attracted attention if the perpetrator was seen leaving."

"What about the film?"

"Film?"

"Actually, I'm sorry, Mr. Haley shot in digital. Did you find the digital cards, or his computer, or his backup hard drive?"

"No."

"Did you find them in Mr. Gamble's yard?" I ask.

"No."

"Any theories why not?"

He shakes his head. "I couldn't say."

"Do you know what was on the missing video?"

"No."

"Could it have been something the killer was afraid of?"

"I have no evidence to that effect."

"Sounds like you looked really hard for it."

Before I let Crenshaw off the stand, I show him a map of the outside of Joey's house, demonstrating that someone could be behind his garage and be undetected by someone in the house. Crenshaw doesn't quite go that far, but agrees that it's possible.

At its core the case is exactly what it seemed to be when it started. Joey has been placed at the murder/robbery scene and had the stolen items and murder weapon in his possession.

In the world of prosecutors, that's about as good as it gets.

There is a heightened feeling of tension in the courtroom today.

That frequently happens when the prosecution has completed their case and the defense is about to begin. Jurors and onlookers have basically heard nothing positive from our side, and they sense that this is the moment we have to put up or shut up.

My guess is that most are betting on us shutting up.

I've taken to nodding hello to Cynthia Gamble, Joey's grandmother, in her first-row seat every morning. She always nods back, but never looks particularly happy about it. She is smart enough to know that while we have picked at the prosecution witnesses with varying degrees of success, we haven't laid a glove on the crux of their case.

This time when I nod, she stands and comes over to me. "I hope you're ready," she says.

I nod. "You and me both."

"Time to stop making debating points and start changing minds."

This is one smart, tough lady.

Our defense strategy falls into three distinct areas. One is the traditional one, trying to create reasonable doubt that Joey did the crime based on the available facts and evidence. That has already proven to be difficult, if not impossible.

Joey was at the scene and had the murder weapon and stolen items in his possession. He has no alibi, no witnesses to swear he was at a birthday party or board meeting while the killing was taking place.

The second area concerns George Adams. There will be no problem with admissibility, and the fact that Adams was himself a violent criminal certainly works in our favor. But while Laurie and I don't believe in coincidences and therefore don't believe that Truman just happened to wind up in the hands of a murderer, that doesn't necessarily mean the jury shares our coincidence aversion.

The third area is simultaneously the most promising and most difficult. This concerns Florida and drugs and Chico Simmons and Frank Silvio and all the tentacles that spread from them. I have no doubt in my mind that whatever Haley learned in Florida provided the motive for his murder, but I so far cannot make any connection between all of that and our case. Until I can, the jury will not hear a word of it.

I have so far received no response from Cindy or the DEA about my insistence on information before I agree to meet with them. Marcus has also had nothing eventful to report from his vantage point in Florida. Those are things I cannot control; all I can do is wait.

But the defense we mount is something I can control, and it starts as Judge Matthews looks at me and says, "Call your first witness."

Here goes.

I call Debra Drake, Dr. Dowling's receptionist, to the stand. After identifying her and describing her occupation, I introduce as evidence a photograph of George Adams. "Have you ever met this person?" I ask.

She nods. "Yes. He brought in a dog and requested that he be euthanized. It was a French bulldog, and he said his name was Buster."

"Was he a regular client?"

"No, he had never been in our office before. Nor had that dog."

"Did he pay for the euthanization and sign a form?"

"Yes," she says. "He paid one hundred ninety-five dollars in cash and signed the form 'Charlie Henderson.'"

I introduce the signed euthanasia form, have her identify it, and then let her off the stand.

Dylan asks how long "Henderson" was in the office.

"Not more than five minutes. Maybe not even that long," Debra says.

"But you're positive you can identify him?"

She nods. "Yes, sir. He was a gruff, scary person, so he made an impression on me."

Next I call Dr. Dowling, who basically tells the exact story he told me that first day in his office, except for the part about Tara being "fine, really fine." He describes scanning the microchip embedded in the dog and eventually learning that his real owner was James Haley, and that the dog's real name was Truman.

"And then I made the connection that Mr. Haley was the man who was murdered that week, so I talked to you about it."

"What did I tell you?" I ask.

"Under no circumstances was I to kill Truman."

The jury and onlookers laugh at that. "And did you?" I ask.

"No, he's safe."

Dylan goes at Dowling a bit harder than he did Debra. "Dr. Dowling, this man who brought Truman into your office, did he say how he got possession of him?"

"No. He claimed to be the owner."

"Could he have found him stray?" Dylan asks.

"I have no idea."

"Here is a hypothetical; tell me if it's possible. Someone broke into Mr. Haley's house, killed him, and left the back door open. The dog then ran out the back door and someone else found him. Is that possible?"

"I suppose, but that's really not my area of expertise."

"I understand, but isn't that what stray dogs are? Dogs that have run off and are found by someone who is not their owner?"

"But why would he pay to have him killed?" Dowling asks. "He could have just taken him to a shelter." If he wasn't already, the response makes Dowling my favorite all-time vet. Dylan gets the remark stricken from the record as unresponsive, but the damage is done.

Next I call Carol Mehlman, twin sister of

Adams's murdered wife, Denise. I think I have already done a lot to establish the fact that Adams had taken Truman, but Carol's testimony furthers that cause. Carol shows the photograph of the dog that her sister emailed to her and explains how Denise had told her George said he was bringing the dog home to her.

That didn't quite work out.

Last up today is Sergeant Jack Rubin from Philadelphia. He came to town last night and had dinner with Laurie and me. They dragged me to a seafood restaurant and they each had a dozen oysters, sucking down those disgusting things with what seemed like great pleasure.

I would not eat an oyster under penalty of death, and I said so.

"You need to be willing to move out of your comfort zone," Laurie had said, as Rubin nodded his agreement.

"It is comfortable in my comfort zone," I said. "The reason I even maintain a comfort zone is because I find it comforting. I'm sorry if that makes you uncomfortable."

"Is he always like this?" Rubin asked.

Laurie nodded. "Pretty much."

"That's a shame," Rubin said.

Rubin proves to be a better witness than he was a dinner companion. My goal is for him to convey to the jury that Adams was a murderer for organized crime in Philadelphia, and he does that completely and colorfully.

"This was a really bad guy," Rubin says, summing up. "There were no cops as pallbearers at his funeral, that I can tell you."

"He's dead?" I ask, feigning surprise.

Before Dylan can object, Rubin says, "He was murdered last month; his body turned up in the Passaic River." Then, "I can think of bigger tragedies."

"Just curious," I say. "When Mr. Adams was murdered, was Mr. Gamble already sitting in jail as a result of being charged in this case?"

"Yes."

"So he's not a suspect?"

Rubin smiles. "I would think not."

Tara leads the life she wants and one that I aspire to.

She is surrounded all day by those she loves and who love her, she has absolutely no responsibilities, she takes leisurely walks in the park, she never has to get dressed up, and she has all her meals served to her.

I think the reason our lives went in such different directions goes back to a crucial youthful decision we both made. I decided to go to law school, and she decided not to.

That is why I am stressed out at having the life of a young, innocent man in my legal hands. I need to find a way to save him, which also will have the side benefit of preventing his grandmother from killing me. If I fail, if they take Joey Gamble away and lock him up for the rest of his life, I am going to have a hell of a lot of trouble living with it, and with myself.

Today is our version of forensics day. First

up is Rob Flory, the ex-forensics cop and the member of our team who took the fingerprints off the euthanasia form. He identifies the prints on the form as belonging to George Adams. He's a very professional, very credible witness, and I'm quite sure his testimony firmly proves the fact that George Adams had James Haley's dog, Truman.

I let Flory off the stand briefly, with instructions that he is still under oath and will be recalled shortly. My next witness is Tommy Halitzky, manager of the Park Village apartments in Hawthorne. He is there simply to confirm that George Adams stayed there and that he used the name Charlie Henderson, the same name he used at Dowling's office, to rent an apartment.

Rob Flory comes back to describe his forensic examination of Adams's apartment. He found Adams's fingerprints, as he had also done on the euthanasia form, and he also recovered dog hair from the apartment and did DNA lab tests on it.

I smile. "Did you find a match?"

"Yes. I also tested hair from the dog known as Truman. The hair in Adams's apartment was definitely Truman's."

Next I call Mark Jamieson, the former Paterson police lieutenant who had joined our team, along with Rob Flory, for the inspection of Adams's apartment.

He describes exactly what went on and says that it was all captured on video, should the court want to see it. He then says that we found Adams's phone. "It was hidden under clothing in a drawer."

"Did you examine the phone?" I ask.

"Eventually, yes," he says, and then talks about the photograph of Frank Silvio and newspaper accounts that Adams had hidden in the Cloud.

Dylan's cross of Jamieson is low-key, as was his cross of Flory, and he acts sort of bemused by all this. His basic approach is that this is all interesting, but what the hell does it have to do with the murder of James Haley?

It's a good question, and one Jamieson and Flory can't effectively answer. It's going to be hard to expect the jury to answer it either.

On redirect, I ask Jamieson if he knows where Frank Silvio is.

"He's dead," he says. "Murdered just a few days ago."

I repeat the questions I had for Rob Flory about George Adams. "Just curious," I say. "When Mr. Silvio was murdered, was Mr. Gamble already sitting in jail as a result of being charged in this case?"

"Yes."

"And his being in jail would be a pretty good alibi as it relates to Mr. Silvio's murder, would it not?"

He nods. "I would say so."

I want the jury to know that people are dropping like flies here, that there are real murderers out on the street, hovering over this case.

I think I'm successfully making that point.

When the court day ends, I turn on my cell phone and play a message from Cindy Spodek, asking me to call her, which I do.

"Andy, I can't believe I'm even saying this, but the DEA did exactly what you want."

"I'm well respected in the law enforcement community," I say. "Admired and revered."

"You're a pain in the ass," she says. "And everybody knows it. But you do seem to have them over a barrel, and I suggest you deliver the goods."

"It all depends on what's in the material. When will I have it?"

"It's being couriered to you today. It might be at your house already."

As soon as I hang up, I call Janet Carlson, heretofore known as the best-looking coroner in America. "Janet, I need you desperately."

She laughs. "That's been said to me a number of times, Andy, and it never ends well."

"What are you doing tonight?"

Another laugh. "That usually doesn't work out either. Are you and Laurie having issues?"

"No, this is work-related, and it is life-or-death important. Can you come over? Laurie will be there to protect you, and you can have anything you want for dinner."

"Is this related to the death of that homeless man that we talked about? There are still issues there that trouble me."

"It's about that and much more," I say. "You can be a hero."

"Okay, I'm intrigued and I'll come over."

"Great. What do you want for dinner?" I ask.

"Prime rib, baked potato, and crème brûlée for dessert."

"We're having pizza."

"Perfect."

Janet has been in my office for two hours.

After Laurie and I told her what we were looking for, she retreated in there with all the information the DEA had accumulated on the other murders around the country. It included autopsy reports and toxicology results. I also received a report as to when each person was last seen before his body was discovered, but that is not something that concerns Janet.

I brought the pizza in to her when it arrived, but she barely looked up, so I got the hell out of here. I don't want to distract her in any way; the answer that she comes out of there with will be the answer to everything.

So all we can do is wait and go about our business. We tuck Ricky into bed and I take Tara and Sebastian on their nighttime walk. I make it a fairly short one, in case Janet finishes. I'm as anxious to hear her verdict as I am to hear the verdict at the end of a trial.

Five minutes after I get back, the door to my office opens and Janet is standing there. "This is simply amazing," she says.

An hour later, after she has taken us through the results case by case, Janet leaves with our sincere thanks and four slices of cold pizza. Laurie and I are just sitting down to discuss our next steps when the phone rings.

I answer it, and it's Cindy Spodek. "I'm not sure why they always want me to be the contact to you," she says. "I'm either just cursed, or maybe they have this weird idea that I can control you."

"I am putty in your hands," I say.

"Have you gone through the materials?"

"I have, and I'm ready to meet with the DEA."

"Good," she says. "Tomorrow?"

"I can't tomorrow; it's Friday and I'm in court. How about Saturday morning?"

"Can it wait that long? They won't be happy about this; they seem pretty anxious."

"Cindy, I know everything, and I know for a fact it can wait." I don't tell her that the fifth of the month is the target date, based on what Lorna Diaz said about Grobin getting the money, and it's a week away. The more information I can hold to use at the meeting, the better.

I wake up in the morning and take Tara and Sebastian out for a walk. As I walk, I try to focus on the court day ahead. It's mostly a day of biding time; this trial is going to be decided in my meeting tomorrow and in what is to follow.

My first witness is Willis Senack, the cousin of Christopher Tolbert who paid for his funeral. After I set up who he is and the details of Tolbert's death, I ask him if he ever met James Haley.

"Yes. He came to Chris's funeral. I found out later that he wanted to shoot footage of it, but the funeral director didn't give him permission. But I did sit for an interview with him afterward."

"Why was he there?" I ask.

"Well, he said it was part of a film he was doing about living in the inner city. He asked me a bunch of questions about Chris, many of which I couldn't answer because I really didn't know him that well."

"Was there a specific area he was interested in?"

He nods. "Drug usage. He wanted to know if Chris had been involved with drugs, if he had been an addict."

"What was your answer?"

"I told him that to my knowledge he hadn't been."

Dylan doesn't even bother to question Senack; he must be wondering why I bothered to call him. Nothing Senack said has anything to do with Haley's murder, nor does it help Joey in any way.

Next up is Benjamin Smolen, the owner of a sporting goods store in downtown Paterson. Joey has worked for him for the last two years, though the employment obviously ended when Joey was arrested.

Smolen is here as a character witness, and he's a good one. He speaks about Joey's resisting gang influences and wanting to earn enough money to go to college. He presents an impressive portrait of a young man.

Dylan basically shrugs him off, limiting his cross-examination to getting Smolen to admit that he has no idea where Joey was the night of the murder or what happened in Haley's house while Joey was there.

It must feel to Dylan like I'm wrapping up our case, as the level of significance of today's witness has not been very high. I surprise him with a request I have for Judge Matthews just before the lunch break. I ask if we can meet in her chambers, and she schedules that meeting for right after lunch.

When we convene there, I say there is a potentially hugely significant development that will either bear fruit or not over the course of the weekend. I ask that we adjourn until Monday.

"Can you be more specific?" Judge Matthews asks.

"I'm afraid I can't, Your Honor. I don't want to be dramatic about it, but if what is happening were to get out, lives would be endangered."

Dylan smirks. "Glad you don't want to be dramatic."

"Your Honor, I can call some meaningless character witnesses if I need to run out the clock this afternoon. But if we adjourn, then on Monday the case will either take an entirely new turn, or I will rest our case. It all depends on this weekend."

Dylan doesn't bother fighting this; he gains nothing by me putting on the character witnesses. Judge Matthews grants the adjournment for the day, but insists that I be ready one way or another on Monday morning.

It's a promise I am able to make, because by Monday the boat will have sailed, maybe literally.

Mateo Rojas had managed to remain successful, and alive, by being unpredictable.

The target date for the end of the operation — or, in Rojas's eyes, the beginning of the operation — had long been October 5. But in Rojas's view it was never carved in stone, and it was about to change.

There were three main factors in Rojas moving things forward. For one, the preparation had gone more smoothly than anticipated. Everything was ready to go; all he had to do was start the process and literally pull the trigger.

The second factor was the death of the fourth crewman, whose body had washed up on shore. It had still not been determined who had killed the crewman, but whoever it was represented a threat to the operation. They represented an unknown, and Rojas much preferred knowns.

Finally, there was the death of Frank Silvio. It had made the crewmen of the *Ginny May* nervous. Silvio was their boss, and more than that, they feared him and his power. If Silvio was vulnerable, and could be killed by someone more fearsome, that was very frightening to them. In their fear, Rojas knew, they could panic and do something to jeopardize the operation at a very sensitive time.

Rojas trusted his instincts, always and completely. And in this situation they told him that other threats might be out there as well, and waiting would only give them more time and opportunity to materialize.

He had no way of knowing how right those instincts were again, or that at that very moment, a meeting was going on in Newark, New Jersey, that could change everything.

Rojas called Bryce Dorsey, whom he had not seen or talked to since the beginning of the operation. He told him that they were kicking the final plan into action that morning, and the three crewmembers were to assemble at the warehouse. The good news, Rojas pointed out, was that their paydays were moving up as well.

The crewmen showed up as directed and spent three hours loading the goods. Rojas pitched in as well; he was not opposed to doing hard work, as long as it could speed things to their conclusion.

When it was over, Rojas lined them up and calmly shot them each in the head. They had known what they were getting into, what they were doing, and what the potential rewards were. What they had failed to realize, until it was too late, was who they were dealing with.

Rojas did not give them a second thought. All he was focused on was completing some paperwork, finalizing some plans, and going on his way.

The meeting is at the DEA office on Mulberry Street in Newark.

Four DEA people are waiting there when I arrive. One is Stephen Watts, the principal deputy administrator, based in Washington. His presence alone is an indicator that they view this as being of the highest importance. Also there are Natalie Brookshier, the special agent in charge of the New Jersey Division, and two other agents who are under Agent Brookshier.

Cindy Spodek has come down as well. She will be a combination representative of the FBI and babysitter for me. She may even have brought along a pacifier.

Watts defers to Brookshier to run the meeting. She thanks me for coming and starts by asking me why I was asking about amephrotane.

Instead I turn to Cindy. "Would you like

to explain the quid-pro-quo situation to them?"

She nods and turns to them. "Andy's a pain in the ass."

"Thanks, Cindy, I'll take it from here. In this case, it's very simple," I say to Brookshier. "I tell you what I know. If it turns out that I am right — and believe me, I am right — then it's going to be huge for you. In return, I require that you come forward, tell the truth, and help me defend my client, who is innocent."

Brookshier nods. "If it's as you say."

"Good. Now, I have one question. Who in your organization did James Haley contact?"

Based on Brookshier's reaction, I can see that I've hit a nerve already, always a good way to start a meeting. She turns to Watts, who silently nods his okay.

"He spoke to an agent in the Washington office. He said that he had huge news about a drug ring that was going to be the biggest drug story in years, maybe forever. He would share it, if he could have the entire exclusive on it. He was making a movie. He wanted us to cooperate, to do on-camera interviews."

"What did the agent say?"

"That we get a number of claims like this, and that when Haley had something solid, he should come to us with it. That we couldn't make any promises until we saw his evidence. How did you know about this?"

"I didn't know for sure, but Haley had a rental car in New Jersey and was planning to return it in Washington. It fit with everything else I know."

"I think it might be time to hear what you know," she says.

"Almost," I say. "I sent Cindy a photograph of a guy that she showed to you. Who is he?"

"The name he goes by is Mateo Rojas. There's no reason to go into the details now, but suffice it to say that he is an international drug criminal and an extraordinarily dangerous individual. If he is involved, the matter is very serious. Let's start there. Why did you have his photograph?"

"It was taken outside a vacant strip mall store. He had just murdered Frank Silvio, a Paterson gang leader named Chico Simmons, and one of his lieutenants. When I leave here, I will be reporting that fact to the Paterson police. I sent it to you because I assumed he was involved in this, but I have no personal knowledge of what his role is."

Watts speaks for the first time since the meeting started. "Just what do you have personal knowledge of?"

I've given a lot of thought to what I should tell them, and I've opted to limit it to the conspiracy itself. There's no need to talk about Chico Simmons or George Adams; they are peripheral players in this. And I'm certainly not going to mention Marcus dispatching the crewmember who attacked Lorna Diaz.

"There's a sponge-diving boat in Wilton Keys, Florida, called the *Ginny May.* It takes tourists out every day while the crew dives. They are somehow retrieving drugs and bringing them to shore; with the tourists on board, there's no reason anyone would be suspicious. And I'm pretty sure at least one member of the local police force is corrupt."

"Where are they getting the drugs from?"

"I suspect a ship is dropping them into the water; it's said to be only eighty feet deep there. The drugs are probably weighted down, and I'm sure they are encased in what looks like natural sponge. The smugglers behind all this, and I assume Rojas is a leader in that group, have arranged for distribution outlets for their drug all over the country. In Paterson it was Chico Simmons; in Philadelphia it is Fat Tony Longo. I imagine the recipients of the drugs are paying huge fees for it, much more than they would traditionally pay. I'm sure other local people around the country are doing the same. And I believe the smugglers are also providing some start-up money to people like Chico Simmons, so that they can consolidate their operations and be ready to move on day one."

"People like Chico and Fat Tony haven't had too much difficulty getting drugs in the past. Why would they go along with it?" Brookshier asks.

"It's a new product, very different than any that has preceded it. So they are treating it like any smart company would: they're building up interest and demonstrating its appeal before giving it a national rollout. It could be a video game, or a new type of chalupa . . . doesn't matter . . . the marketing is all the same. It's the new big thing to come along."

"How is it different?" Brookshier asks.

"I'm not sure of all the ways; there could be more," I say. "But for one thing, it is incredibly, almost instantly addictive. And then . . ."

"Oh my God," Cindy says, interrupting, a look of horror on her face.

"What's the matter?" Brookshier asks.

"Did you read the material you sent Andy? Did you even read it?"

"Does somebody want to explain this?" Watts asks.

I turn to Cindy. "You want to take it?"

"These murder victims . . . the homeless men," she says, the horror still evident on her face. "They were guinea pigs . . . they were experiments."

Everybody just stares at her, so she continues. "Don't you see? None of them had prior drug use; that's why they were chosen. The demonstration was to show how quickly they could get them addicted. It was one of the selling points of the new product. It's in the autopsies; they all showed signs that could indicate the victims had experienced withdrawal."

I nod. "I've had a coroner go over the autopsies you provided me. She's positive that I'm right about this. You could have your experts examine it as well, but they will come to the same conclusion, and by then it will be too late."

"What else did you learn?"

"That the drug quickly breaks down in the system; that's why there were no traces of anything other than the amephrotane," I say. "So it's highly addictive and the need for more is almost immediate. The ideal new product."

"Shit," Watts says.

"I'm sure there must be other aspects that make it so desirable. For example, I imagine that the quantities necessary are very, very small. That's why so much could be brought in by one boat, even though it was over time."

"Where is all of it now?"

"My investigation shows it is in a warehouse outside of Wilton Keys. The warehouse has very substantial surveillance and alarm capabilities, much more than would be needed to protect a bunch of sponges. I have reason to believe it is not shipping out until around the fifth of the month."

"You're positive about this?" Brookshier asks.

"I haven't seen the drugs, if that's what you mean, but I'm positive. There simply cannot be another explanation."

"He's right," Cindy says.

"You have the location?" Brookshier asks.

"I do."

"And Haley learned about this?"

I nod. "He certainly knew about a lot of it. I can demonstrate how I know this, but it's not essential for this meeting. I don't know if he knew all the details, but it was enough to get him killed."

Just then my cell phone rings; I had meant to turn it off, but forgot. I glance at it and see that it's Laurie. "It's Laurie," I say to Cindy. "She knows I'm here and wouldn't be calling if it weren't important."

I answer the call and Laurie says, "Willie just called. Marcus asked him to tell you there's activity at the warehouse. The guy who killed Silvio and Chico is there. He thinks they're about to move out."

Willie hung up after Laurie said she would contact Andy and call him right back.

Marcus had moved closer to the warehouse to get a better look at what was going on. There had not been any sign of activity in the place for a while, but they knew the four people were still in there.

Marcus had stayed in Willie's line of vision while Willie was on the phone, but then suddenly he was gone. Willie had no idea what happened to him, whether he had gone around the back or inside.

He decided he couldn't sit there and wait for Laurie to call back; he had to find out what happened to Marcus. Four against one was daunting, even for Marcus. Four against two, when the two were Marcus and Willie, was a fair fight, no matter who the four were.

So Willie turned off his phone ringer and started for the warehouse.

I turn to the others in the room and quickly tell them what Laurie said.

"We need to get people there right away," is Watts's response. "If they get on the open road, we may never find them."

"Unless they're moving the stuff by boat," Brookshier says.

I shake my head. "Doesn't make sense. They'd have to sneak it into the country again. It's already here; why would they go through that process again?"

Watts turns to an agent and says, "Get assets down there," and the agent gets up to put that into action.

"I have people there; they are capable of stopping this," I say. "Should I send them in?"

"No," Watts says. "Tell them to wait for our people."

"That could be too late," I say. "If they get it out of the warehouse, the whole balance of power changes."

"Is Marcus one of the people?" Cindy asks.

I nod. "And Willie."

"On behalf of the Bureau, I say send them in."

"You have no idea how dangerous Rojas is," Brookshier says.

I turn back to the phone and say to Laurie, "Send them in, but tell Marcus that Rojas is incredibly dangerous." She then asks a question, which I put to the people in the room.

"Is it okay if Marcus has to kill Rojas, or must he keep him alive?" I don't wait for an answer; I just tell Laurie, "Whatever he needs to do."

I hang up so Laurie can call Willie back. I'm expecting we're going to have wait a long time to hear what happened. As confident as I am in Marcus and Willie, this is the most scared I have been in a long time.

But we have a very short wait — not more than three minutes — until Laurie calls back.

"Willie's not answering his phone," she says.

"Shit," I say.

The warehouse had an elaborate security system, including cameras.

That is how we were able to see exactly how events unfolded within two hours after they happened. Laurie had finally heard back from Willie and Marcus and called to report how it went down. Then DEA agents descended on the scene, secured the video, and transmitted it up here.

There's no way, just based on the video, to know how Marcus got inside the warehouse. It's entirely possible, since Rojas and the others were inside, that they had just left the door open.

There is also no way to know how the three crewmen were killed, but we can see their bodies lying on the floor. I can only assume that Rojas killed them, since, in his eyes, they obviously knew too much, and he no longer needed them.

But we can see Rojas coming off the truck,

then being lifted off his feet by Marcus and thrown back against the truck. We can see him reach for his gun, but Marcus is too quick for him, chopping down on Rojas's arm.

And then Marcus backs off a few feet, as if inviting Rojas to come at him. There is no audio on the tape, so even though we can see that they are talking, we can't know what is being said. Of course, I can't imagine that Rojas could understand what Marcus was saying anyway; I never can.

"Doesn't he carry a gun?" Brookshier asks. When I say that he does, she asks, "So what is he doing?"

"He's being Marcus," Cindy says.

So Rojas does go at him. He looks like he knows how to fight and is extremely dangerous, as advertised. Marcus completely dismantles him; it seems like it takes ten seconds, but it might be a little longer.

"Wow," says Brookshier.

I smile. "That's my little Markie."

When it's over, Rojas is lying motionless on the floor. It's hard to know whether he is alive or dead, and the truth is that I don't give a shit. Willie comes into the screen and says something to Marcus, and the tape cuts off.

371

I turn to the others in the room. "Now for the quid pro quo."

I'm setting my goals higher now.

Originally, my goal had been to get testimony about the drug conspiracy in front of the jury. That would have established the fact that Haley knew things about very bad and dangerous people, and would have demonstrated that they had a motive to murder him.

But if that's all I get out of this, then Joey's fate will still be in the hands of the jury. They will weigh the evidence about Adams and the Florida drug situation, which might seem weird and confusing and distant, against the very real and concrete forensic evidence against Joey.

So in this meeting in Judge Matthews's chambers, I want more. Present are the judge, Dylan, Dylan's assistant counsel, Agent Brookshier of the DEA, Cindy Spodek, Hike, and myself.

Hike wrote an outstanding brief and had

it delivered to the court and opposing counsel yesterday. It brilliantly lays out exactly what happened, and our theory of the case. By design, it does not speak to our desire to get the evidence admitted at trial, for one main reason.

We want more.

Judge Matthews reads into the record the list of people present and then turns the floor over to me.

"I know you've read the brief," I say, "so I won't repeat it chapter and verse. But I do want to hit the high points." I go on and do just that, making the connections I had never been able to make before, between Chico Simmons and George Adams and Frank Silvio and Florida.

"They were all part of the same conspiracy," I say, "a conspiracy that James Haley had discovered and was about to expose. So they killed him and framed Joey Gamble. Chico Simmons gave George Adams Joey's head on a silver platter."

I turn the floor over to Brookshier, saying that I will finish after she has her say. And boy, does she have her say.

"You know all the details of what happened here," she says. "We are still learning about the conspiracy and about the new drug, all of which has been confiscated. But

I am here to say that James Haley was a hero, and that is how he died. He was not a victim of a robbery/homicide by Joey Gamble.

"It is the official position of the Drug Enforcement Administration, and of the Federal Bureau of Investigation" — she glances at a nodding Cindy as she says this — "and of the United States Government that Joseph Gamble is innocent of the crime for which he is being tried.

"Should he somehow be convicted of this crime, the Justice Department will file an immediate brief in support of his appeal. Thank you."

I thank Brookshier; there's a woman who knows the meaning of "quid pro quo." Then I try to close the sale.

"Your Honor, Dylan, this is not a case that should go to the jury. I am not worried that my client will be convicted; we all know that with these developments, that is not going to happen. But if so much as one of the jurors can't see the big picture here and hangs the jury, it will damage Joey Gamble's life and reputation forever.

"They only picked Joey to frame because Chico Simmons had been told that Joey was going to be at Haley's that night. It made him the perfect candidate to set up.

"Please do the right thing and end this now."

Judge Matthews thinks about this for a few moments, then says, "I am inclined to order a directed verdict of acquittal. But that requires the evidentiary reasons for my decision to be submitted into the record."

Brookshier shakes her head. "We would be opposed to that, Your Honor. Some of this material is very sensitive; it may even wind up classified."

The judge turns to Dylan. "Mr. Campbell?"

Dylan doesn't hesitate. He says, "We will move to dismiss the charges."

"Can we make it clear publicly that this is not a question of reasonable doubt, but in fact an affirmation of Joey's innocence?" I ask.

"I'm on it," Dylan says.

So we go into court and Judge Matthews calls the jury in. The first thing she does is call on Dylan, who stands and says, "Your Honor, as you are aware, some major new developments have come to light, and I would therefore like to announce on behalf of the State of New Jersey that all charges against Mr. Joseph Gamble are hereby dismissed."

Pretty much everyone sits in stunned

silence, and the jurors all look at one another not knowing what the hell is going on. Joey turns to me and asks, "What does that mean?"

"It means that sitting behind you is one happy grandmother."

So I stand up and turn back to Cynthia Gamble. She's in the process of hugging Laurie, but finally breaks it off and moves toward me. Then I am the recipient of my first-ever grandmother high five, followed by a hell of a hug.

Who said I'm not good with grandmothers?

We wait in court for Joey to get his papers processed, and then Joey, Cynthia, Hike, Laurie, and I leave the courtroom and go outside. I'm surprised to see that microphones have been brought onto the courthouse steps, and Dylan is giving a brief talk to the assembled press and onlookers.

"I don't want there to be any confusion about this," Dylan says. "And I want what I am saying to be on every TV station and in every newspaper." He pauses, then says, "This was no technicality. This young man, Joey Gamble, is completely, totally, and absolutely innocent. If we knew then what we know now, he never would have been charged. He has my sincere apology for the nightmare he has been through."

I make my way to Dylan and he leans over to me when I get close. "Dylan, you know that scene at the end of *Karate Kid,* where the guy who lost the match comes over and hands the winner the trophy and says, 'You're okay, LaRusso'?"

He shakes his head. "No, never saw it."

"Doesn't matter," I say. "The point is, you're okay, Campbell."

And we shake hands.

As always, we have our victory party at Charlie's Sports Bar.

It's slightly different in that this time, our victorious client is not old enough to drink, but some traditions are too important to change.

Laurie and I are the hosts, and the guests are Willie, Sondra, Hike, Edna, Sam, Marcus, Cindy Spodek, Joey Gamble, and his grandmother Cynthia. Ricky's here as well, which is why the party is starting at six o'clock.

Vince Sanders and Pete Stanton are also here, because the food and beer are free, and like every night, they are thirsty and hungry and cheap.

Cindy has stayed in the area for a few days to wrap up the FBI's part in this, and she has updated us on law enforcement's progress.

The developments have been considerable. Marcus did not kill Rojas at the warehouse, fortunately, and between recovered documentation and Rojas's willingness to talk, arrests of the potential recipients of the drugs are being made around the country. According to Cindy, the DEA is also making efforts to destroy the production source, which is out of the country, though she does not know where or how they are planning to do that.

It turns out that Mike Morrison, the cop in Wilton Keys who I'd thought was corrupt, was not. However, his maritime officer, the one who helped fake Silvio's death on the boat, was dirty as hell.

Edna approaches me and says that she wants to rescind her retirement threat. "I was under stress," she says. "You had just taken on a client, which was upsetting. But I've rethought it, and I want to stay on the team."

"Edna," I say, "I'm glad to hear this. I had no idea how we were going replace you."

Marcus, for his part, spends the night showing everyone photos of his new daughter, all the while grinning like a happy new father. That is probably because he's a happy, new father.

As the party is nearing a conclusion, Laurie taps her glass with a spoon to get everyone's attention. "Andy has something to say," she says.

I shake my head. "It was your idea, so you should make the announcement."

She nods. "Okay. Lost in all of this is the fact that James Haley was a real journalist and a real hero. He uncovered a terrible conspiracy, and he was going to expose it. And he lost his life in the effort."

Total silence in the room; this is so far not really upbeat party talk.

"So Andy and I would like to announce that we are creating the James Haley Award, which is a four-year college scholarship in his honor. Tuition, room, and board. The first recipient, we are delighted to say, is Joey Gamble."

Everyone cheers and raises their glasses in a toast to Joey, who is stunned into silence. Cynthia Gamble sits off to the side, softly sobbing.

I go over to her and sit next to her. "Are you okay?"

She nods and composes herself. "This is the greatest night of my life. Thank you."

I start to formulate some joking response, but I hold on to it. This is just not the time to joke, even for me.

"I want to ask you a question," she finally says.

"Anything."

"Joey's going to be off to college — I can't even believe I'm saying those words. But he will be, and for the first time, really in my life, I'll be all alone. So I was thinking, I'd like to get a dog."

I smile. "I can take care of that. What kind of dog are you looking for?"

She shakes her head slightly. "I want Truman. I want to take care of Mr. Haley's dog and give him a great life."

I smile again, wider this time. "I can take care of that too."

ABOUT THE AUTHOR

David Rosenfelt is the Edgar-nominated and Shamus Award-winning author of eleven stand-alones and eighteen Andy Carpenter novels, most recently *Deck the Hounds.* After years of living in California, he and his wife moved to Maine with twenty-five of the four thousand dogs they have rescued.